A BLESSING IN DISGUISE

A Blessing in Disguise

□ ■ □

Eleanora E. Tate

DELACORTE PRESS

Published by
Delacorte Press
Bantam Doubleday Dell Publishing Group, Inc.
1540 Broadway
New York, New York 10036

The text of this book was set in 12-point Berling.

Library of Congress Cataloging in Publication Data

Tate, Eleanora E.
A blessing in disguise / by Eleanora E. Tate.
p. cm.
Summary: Twelve-year-old Zambia thinks that life with her aunt and uncle in Deacons Neck, South Carolina, is boring and dreams of going to live with her smooth-talking, fast-living father, until she gets to know the darker side of his world.
ISBN 0-385-32103-1
[1. Afro-Americans—Fiction. 2. Fathers and daughters—Fiction. 3. Family life—Fiction. 4. Drug traffic—Fiction.] I. Title.
PZ7.T21117Bl 1995
[Fic]—dc20 94-13073
CIP
AC

Manufactured in the United States of America

February 1995

10 9 8 7 6 5 4 3 2 1

BVG

This book is dedicated to
Charlotte Sheedy

C • H • A • P • T • E • R

1

Check this out: Here I was again, on the Friday afternoon of Fourth of July weekend. I had nothing to do again but sit on my bike in the middle of dull, dusty Silver Dollar Road. Worse, I was still in itsy-bitsy, countrified, do-nothing Deacons Neck, South Carolina. I hadn't even heard a single firecracker explode. I wished my father would take me to his nightclub at the beach.

My best friend, Lupe Gore, and my cousin, Aretha Twiggins, were on their bikes with me, being bored too. "I haven't even seen a dog cross the road," I said. "I bet everybody's in Gumbo Grove or Myrtle Beach—but us."

"You never see cars or anything happening on this street," Lupe said. "At least I get to go to Gumbo Grove tonight, even if it is only to that old folks' lodge barbecue."

"What barbecue?" I asked.

"The Ezekiel Crown Lodge barbecue, Zambia. Aren't you going? Your folks are in the lodge." Lupe popped her gum at us. "Didn't they tell you? Maybe you're gonna have to stay home. You act so country out in public, anyway."

"Who's country?" Aretha said. "Zambia, Momma told us about that barbecue, didn't she? Didn't Daddy?"

"No. All I've heard from Uncle Lamar and Aunt Limo is 'county fair, county fair,' " I said. "I don't wanna go to *nobody's* county fair on the Fourth of July weekend when I could be in Gumbo Grove and—"

"Go shopping at the beachwear stores," Lupe said.

"Go wading in that ocean," Aretha added.

"Go looking for cuties at my daddy's Paradise Number One!" I clapped my hands and wiggled my head. "I'd die to get inside there tonight. I hear it stays boss twenty-four seven."

"Twenty-four seven? Nobody says that anymore, Zambia," Lupe said. "Just you country folks. Nobody says it on *Soul Train* or BET."

"They do too," I said back. Had I been watching reruns? "Wish I was born in New York or L.A. I'd be a movie star or a rapper by now."

"Dream on," said Aretha. "You could be in New York or L.A., but you'd still be in remedial math, trying to move up to the front of the room."

Aretha and Lupe did high fives. *"Sí, sí, señorita!"* said Lupe. Lupe had Spanish in her, see, on her mother's side. She liked to try to speak it, even though the closest she'd ever been south of the border was to South of the Border, South Carolina, that Mexican tourist theme park.

"So go ahead and laugh," I said. "I wanna get to Paradise now!" Paradise Number One was the hottest black nightclub in Gumbo Grove, and my daddy,

Vernon "Snake" LaRange, owned it. My daddy was rich, wore expensive clothes, drove fine rides, and *all* the ladies thought he was handsome. To me, he looked just like Nino from that movie *New Jack City*. One of these days I was going to live with Snake and be rich too! For now I had to settle for my dull cousin Aretha, old dull Uncle Lamar, and old-fashioned Aunt Limousine.

Uncle Lamar was so dull that if he stood by my daddy, my daddy's flash would make Uncle Lamar disappear. My daddy was tall and slender. Uncle Lamar was short and kind of fat, and always wore plain white shirts and brown or black pants and those thick-soled black shoes. My daddy could shake his head and snap his fingers certain ways—with style! Uncle Lamar just chewed on his lip and snored.

"What time does this barbecue start?" I asked.

"Six or seven." Lupe looked at her watch. "It's after four now. I gotta get ready. Hope you *señoritas* can go."

I looked back toward our house and slid my right foot onto my bike pedal. "Come on, Aretha." I took off. "I'm checking out this barbecue thing with Aunt Limo right now. I know she's home from work. They *can* do good barbecue at those things."

I resigned myself to the barbecue because I knew better than to even think about strutting into Snake's nightclub. Lupe, Aretha, and I were only twelve. A lot of other kids our age went in, but my folks would skin me alive if I did. Didn't matter to Aunt Limo that Snake was her baby brother either.

I dropped my bike down in the driveway by Uncle

Lamar's old junky rattletrap blue Datsun and hopped up on the porch. "Aunt Limo, you home?" I called. When I didn't see her in the living room, I swung around to the kitchen, where Aunt Limo was setting a pot on the stove. Her name was Limousine for real too. She was real short and slender, and she had dark skin and light-brown eyes, like Snake and I did. And Aunt Limo could be cool—even if she was behind the times. I guess she was that way because Uncle Lamar was. If it wasn't for her, I'd go crazy in this old dead house.

The pot looked as big as her head. "Aunt Limo? Hey, Aunt Limo, how come you and Uncle Lamar's going to a barbecue tonight on the beach and we don't know about it?"

"Zambia Renelda Brown, I told you and Aretha both!"

"Uh-uh!"

"Did too! But you said this one would be dead because it was going to be out at Cuffy's Island, like it was on Memorial Day. Remember how Aretha complained about the mosquitoes and how scared she was of the dark? How you said alligators were gonna crawl out of the swamp and pull you in?" She looked at me. "So why're you wanting to go now?"

I shrugged. " 'Cause Lupe said it's gonna be at the lodge in Gumbo Grove now." I grinned sideways at her.

Aunt Limo edged over to me and pushed me a little with her hip. "But it'll still have mosquitoes and be dark."

I hipped her back. "But it won't be boring. Can we go?"

"Of course! But listen." She waggled her spoon at me. "You and Aretha stay away from *that club*, you hear? Don't even mention it around Lamar!"

"I hear." I sucked on my tooth. If she and Uncle Lamar had their way, I'd be ninety years old before I got inside my daddy's club. Uncle Lamar is a recovering alcoholic, see, and he didn't like anybody else drinking liquor either. He didn't smoke and he didn't dance. He didn't do anything fun. He just worked, worked, worked, slept, went to the lodge, and picked paper up out of the yard.

I've lived with my uncle and aunt since I was four, after my mother—Renelda Zambia Brown—got sick and had to go into a hospital in Charleston. She was still in there. Her liver was all messed up from alcohol. Aunt Limo said it did something to her nervous system too. When kids asked what was wrong with her, I said she had cancer.

Every Christmas and on my birthday Aunt Limo handed me cards she said came from Momma. I knew the cards were really from Aunt Limo, because of the handwriting, but I pretended. When Aunt Limo called the hospital, I couldn't bring myself to talk to Momma on the phone. I didn't let myself think too much about her. It made me sad inside when I did.

I thought about my daddy, Snake, a lot. He lived in Gumbo Grove with a lady named Sissy and their two daughters, Meritta and Seritta, twins, my fifteen-year-old half sisters. People said I looked more like Seritta and Snake than Meritta did. In fact, Seritta, Snake, Aunt Limo and I looked just like each other, dark, with light-brown eyes. I liked Seritta a lot. She was always nice to me, no matter where she was. Meritta was light-skinned like her mother, Sissy. She had freckles, a big crooked nose, fat legs, and a big butt. And she was mouthy. Maybe I'd like her more if we lived together.

Later on Aretha and I tore through our clothes, trying to decide on what to wear to the barbecue. Aretha held up a blouse. "I gotta look just right for Garvey Avenue," she said.

"It won't matter what you wear. Won't be a soul looking at you." I wiggled into a pair of jeans and shook my behind at her. "Everybody'll peep at me."

"I guess so," she said. "Peeping at that hole in the butt of those pants."

"Whoa!" I snatched off the pants and looked. It wasn't that big, but Snake's daughter couldn't wear holey clothes!

We took turns working on our hair. Aretha wanted a ponytail and side curls. I wanted curls all over, but the air was so hot and sticky that Aretha couldn't get a curl to hold in my hair. She didn't know any more about hair than I did. I wished I could wear my hair like Meritta and Seritta did, but Aunt Limo wouldn't let me. Extensions hung down their backs in long waves, or in thick shiny black braids. I heard the hair came from China.

"My hair is Aunt Limo's fault," I said. "Wish I could get an extension. Then it'd be so boss, people'd bow down to me on the street, saying, 'The Queen has arrived!' "

"Well, it won't happen tonight." Aretha unsnapped a roller from my hair and dropped it in my lap. "Don't blame Momma. You need to wash your hair more, and brush and oil it more, like she says. I do."

I jammed my black hat on my head and called it quits. "I'm ready. Let's go. It's hot in here."

Out in the front yard we stared up and down the street for signs of life. Miz Arzalia, one of our neighbors, walked up the sidewalk toward us. She was the only thing moving. She carried a cake plate.

"Hope she's coming with us," Aretha whispered. "She always has some juicy gossip."

"Yeah, just as long as it's not about Snake," I said.

"Good evening, ladies," Miz Arzalia said. "This is double chocolate marble cake. I'll save you a piece if you want." We both had to say "yes, thanks" to that.

Aunt Limo pushed open the screen door just then and stepped onto the porch with a large aluminum-foil-covered bowl in her tiny hands. "You're right on time," Aunt Limo told Miz Arzalia. "You can go on and get in the car. You girls get in too."

I slid onto one side of the backseat and Miz Arzalia got in the other side, with Aretha between us. Aunt Limo handed Aretha the bowl.

Uncle Lamar came out in his white shirt and brown pants. He pushed his fat tummy behind the steering wheel and twisted the key in the ignition. Nothing happened, as usual. He jiggled the key, pumped on the gas pedal, scratched the bald spot on the back of his head through his cap, straightened his glasses, and tried again. Still nothing.

Every time he pumped, I'd poke Aretha in the side. The engine finally caught. We clunked off in a column of blue smoke and a clatter of rattles and bangs. We pinged, popped, and backfired the whole fifteen miles to Gumbo Grove in the slow lane in bumper-to-bumper Friday night traffic.

I wanted to brag to Aretha that Snake had three cars and they all drove great, but then she would have come back with, "Yeah, but you haven't been in any of them."

Then I'd have to say something again and then Miz Arzalia would have gotten started. She'd go way back to when Snake was a kid, and how he strangled somebody's prize rabbits, and set some elementary school on fire, and so on. Then she would bring up drugs and stealing and stuff.

She must have read my mind. "I read in the paper that drug traffic at the beach is so common now that the dealers sell it in hotels, on boats, and even in the water. I heard drug dealers are singing in the choirs over there now in both the Baptist *and* the AME churches. And that Snake is a tenor in one of them."

"No!" Aunt Limo and Uncle Lamar said at the same time.

I let out a hard, loud sigh. "Can't they talk about somebody else?" I whispered to Aretha.

"If Snake hasn't turned over a new leaf, he needs to come down out of the choir." Miz Arzalia paid me no attention. "That's going too far."

"Maybe he has," Aunt Limo said. "You never know."

"That's right," I said out loud.

"If you ask me," Uncle Lamar said, "anybody who lies down with dogs will get up with fleas. Snake's into more wrong deals than ever. Besides all that drug dealing, I know for a fact that he has people steal cars from tourists, strip down the cars, then sell the parts all over the county."

"We are sure blessed over here in Deacons Neck," Miz Arzalia said. "Thank God we don't have those kinds of problems anymore."

"Well, let's just hope that it stays that way," Uncle Lamar said.

Uncle Lamar slowed down, turned off of Strom Thurmond Highway onto Garvey Avenue. I heard fast, heavy bass beats coming from the Paradise Number One still half a block away. It'd stay open twenty-four hours a day from now until the Fourth of July holiday ended Monday morning, July fifth.

"C'mon now. Get it! Yeah!" I sang. Aretha and I snapped our fingers and bounced against each other. "Now hit it!"

"Listen to that awful noise." Uncle Lamar made a sucking sound out the side of his mouth like he had something caught in a tooth that he couldn't remove.

"Keep it down, girls," Aunt Limo said. "You're disturbing Uncle Lamar."

"Not them," he said. "I mean that *boom, ba-boom, boom-boom* business coming out of that guy's club, like he's sending out his call to the lowlifes. The slugs'll slide out from under the rocks now, and crawl all over *us* trying to get to the Paradise. Some Paradise."

"Who's a slug?" I sat up. "Who—"

"Hey, anybody can change," Aunt Limo said. "Now, let's just have a good time and quit talking about Snake." She turned around in the seat and smiled a little at me as she spoke. I smiled back a little too. Miz Arzalia and Uncle Lamar shut up. I reminded myself to thank Aunt Limo for that.

A few folks stood around several barbecue grills on the side lawn of Ezekiel Crown No. 147 Star Lodge. Long cream-colored Cadillacs and burgundy Lincoln town cars sat in neat spaces around the front of the building. Lupe swung around the corner just then on her big farm-girl legs. She fluffed out her curly brown hair and pointed. "Meet you at the Peeping Spot." We ran to the landing at the far end of the lodge and arranged ourselves on the steps. Here we could peep and see everything going on outside at the Paradise. Front row seats!

Plus, sitting out here once a month in the summer, waiting for Aunt Limo and Uncle Lamar to get through with lodge business, I even saw my dad sometimes. I'd wave at him and he'd wave back. I hope he knew who I was.

"Sure wish we had something like this on Silver Dollar Road," Lupe said. "We don't even have a club like your dad's in Deacons Neck anywhere."

We only had a barber shop, Reed's Christian Grocery, and a couple of churches on Silver Dollar Road. There wasn't much more in the whole town, besides the mall, some gas stations, and the courthouse. We had pigs and cows and tractors in town, and gardens in everybody's yards. And Miz Arzalia even had chickens. There was one old garage on our street that had been a nightclub, but it had been closed for a million years. There weren't even any other kids on Silver Dollar Road but the Gores and us!

Aretha told Lupe that Miz Arzalia and Uncle Lamar had talked awful about my dad. "I thought Zambia was going to smack Miz Arzalia," Aretha said. "I thought she was gonna go over the seat after Daddy."

"Well, I get tired of all that junk. They wouldn't like it if I lied on *their* relatives right in front of them all the time. I'm glad Aunt Limo said something."

"Well, people go to the Paradise for cutting and shooting and excitement, and for that hot, hot music." Lupe drew up her shoulders and blew a kiss at me. "Otherwise they'd stay home, 'cause it'd be dull—like it is over here. Everybody's just sitting around over here, feeding their faces. They need juice or something to wake them up!"

Just then the Paradise's jukebox took off with a loud crash of drums, guitars, and cymbals. "All right!" Lupe shouted. We jumped off the steps and danced in the grass. We hardly ever heard music loud like this on Silver Dollar Road, unless Potsey rode by with his radio on. Even his didn't last long loud. Uncle Lamar and Miz Arzalia wouldn't allow it. They'd call the police if they heard loud music.

Potsey was Lupe's fine thirteen-year-old brother. I'd been dying to get next to him for years. Potsey, though, didn't pay too much attention to anybody. He just sat back and watched and smiled. I closed my eyes and pretended that I was dancing with Potsey.

When the song ended, we wandered over to the picnic tables and piled up our plates with barbecued ribs, fried chicken, macaroni and cheese, and potato salad, then returned to the landing to eat. We didn't see a single other kid at the barbecue. 'Course, there wouldn't have been many to come anyway, since most of the lodge folks were old and their kids were grown.

Up the street I saw Snake's blue minivan head our way. I hopped off the steps. "You better look out," Lupe called after me. "Seritta's at the wheel."

I ignored Lupe. Seritta wasn't that bad a driver. She wasn't old enough to have a license to drive yet, but that hadn't stopped her. Nobody messed with her or Meritta. They were Snake's girls. Plus, it was Meritta who couldn't drive worth diddly-squat. Seritta turned into Snake's parking lot. Meritta climbed out of the side of the van. I threw on my special smile I used just for them and edged right out to the road where they had to see me.

"Seritta, Daddy told me he's gonna get us new color TVs, American Express credit cards, and take us to Epcot Center in Florida for our birthday," Meritta was saying. She looked straight at me when she said it, too. Neither one of them spoke to me.

I held on to my smile until after they had entered the club. Then I tried to wrestle the disappointment off my face before I returned to the landing. Aretha read my frowned-up face, and steered Lupe around before

Lupe could see it too. "C'mon ladies," she said. "Let's go cop some dessert."

I strolled past people, picking up snatches of old folks' conversations. "Is that Duke Ellington's 'Take the A Train' you're playing?" Uncle Lamar asked Lupe's father, Leon Gore, who was the DJ. "Can't hear it." He cupped his hand to his ear, pointed toward Paradise, then shook his head.

"Then you need to tell your brother-in-law to turn that mess down," Mr. Gore said back.

Miz Arzalia, sitting up under the speaker, patted her foot and chewed at the same time. "Put on some Natalie Cole next, Leon. I just love how she does her daddy's songs."

Not many more lodge people showed up, which disappointed Aunt Limo. "There must have been something good on TV," I heard her tell somebody. "Where is everybody?"

"They might be scared of what's going on across the street," Uncle Lamar said. "You getting enough to eat, sis?" he asked when I walked past. "You know how I like to fill you up." He put another piece of chicken on my plate before I could say no. I liked for him to call me sis. He always wanted me to eat like a pig out in public, so I wouldn't be hungry back home like we were last winter.

He was always saying things like that, or "I gotta take good care of you and get you raised up right." I kind of liked that too, but I wished it was Snake—my dad—saying that instead of him.

The darker and later the night became, the louder

Snake's music got. The bossest Jeeps, Grand Ams, and vans I ever saw in my life, with neon tracer lights going every which way and their car audio systems blasting, rolled up and down the street. The lightbulb at the little ice cream shop next to Snake's cast a circle of light around the door and turned the people milling around a pale yellow. It was like a carnival, with folks everywhere eating and drinking, talking and laughing—across the street.

"This is how the county fair ought to be," Lupe said. "Let's get closer." Humming, we strolled around the lodge property until we strolled right over to the lodge parking lot. Two guys we knew from Deacons Neck Middle School ran past us and, laughing loudly, hopped through the nightclub doors.

"I'll be glad when I have lots of money." I moved away from Aretha and danced to the music. "I'd buy me some fly clothes, a CD, a color TV, and a minivan. No, a Lexus. No, a Jeep Blazer."

Lupe heard me and followed. "Yeah, buying it with play money, and in your dreams."

"No, I'd have real money 'cause I'd have a real job—working for my daddy, Snake."

"Your uncle would tie you to a chair before he'd let you work in a nightclub."

"I'd be grown, so he couldn't stop me. And if I lived with Meritta and Seritta, I could work for Snake now, like they do."

"What's with you and the Two Stooges so much?" Lupe said.

"Don't call them Stooges, Lupe. I've been thinking."

"Thinking? Oh, you're in trouble now."

"No, listen." I lowered my voice so Aretha couldn't hear. "It'd be nice to be around folks who didn't work like slaves and not make a dime. The last time Uncle Lamar gave me some money he crumpled up one of the dollars so tight I had to iron the thing to make it flat again. Then he had to give me a lecture on how to spend it."

"You lie," Lupe laughed. "Look, there they go." We watched a group of guys standing out in front of the nightclub. Every time a car drove by they'd holler, "Yo! Yo!" If it stopped, one of them would run up to the car. "You don't see *that* on Silver Dollar Road either," Lupe said. "I told you they were selling dope. Right out in the open. They must think they're in Atlanta or New York someplace."

"How do you know that that's what they're doing?" I asked.

"I know 'cause my eyes can see 'em doing it. They're sure not selling tacos and crab cakes."

"It's not Snake's fault. He can't control what goes on outside his place. That's how lies about Snake being a drug dealer get started. You sound like Miz Arzalia and Uncle Lamar."

Aretha came over and peered at me. "What're you fussing about? Money again? You gotta get a job first."

"That's why she's watching the dealers," Lupe told her. "So she can learn how to make that easy money.

And then she's gonna move in with her daddy and the Two Stooges, and help the Two Stooges sell drugs."

"Move?" Aretha's voice went high. "Does Momma—"

"Lupe's lying. Their names are not the Two Stooges, and they don't sell drugs." My half sisters was a touchy subject between me and Aretha. "See that dude there, though? He's gone up to four cars already. Wonder what he's really doing."

"Girl, as if you didn't know," Lupe groaned. "Aretha, come get your cousin and tell her the facts of life!"

C · H · A · P · T · E · R

2

By midnight, so many cars tried to drive back and forth on Garvey that they had to take turns. Folks stood along the sidewalk on both sides of Snake's nightclub like they were watching a parade.

And the music! The bass beats from the club and the cars vibrated off the walls of the lodge, nearby houses, and through my bones. At the edge of the street under the streetlight we had a hot lip-synch contest going. On the fast songs my moves hung right with the beat and my lips didn't miss a word. And on the slow songs I swayed, shook my sugar, and waved my arms, just like in the videos. But check this out: Inside my head I was singing to Potsey, and auditioning for Snake.

A man walking by paused. "Do it, mama," he said as he passed on by. I swayed some more for sure then.

Guess what? I won! But when the music cut off suddenly my little thin voice got caught hanging alone in the air. "You may know how to move," Lupe screamed, "but you sure can't sing!" She and Aretha bumped butts.

"Hey! Turn my music back on!" I slapped my hands

to my hips. "Snake, you're ruining my chance to be a star!"

"Look, the DJ just came out the door," said Aretha. "This must be his break time. Let's see what other food's on the tables."

The lodge folks were still in the same seats and still doing the same dull things as they were when we left them. Except for Aunt Limo. She was dancing on the sidewalk with some guy. Lupe pressed her hands over her ears. "Daddy, the music over here is loud now," she hollered.

"I better turn it back down," said Mr. Gore. "Or else somebody'll say we're disturbing the peace and call the cops on us."

Everybody laughed. "Lamar'd be the only person the police could catch to arrest," Miz Arzalia said. "They sure don't know how to catch real criminals, like Snake."

I tightened my lips. "How do you know?" I asked in her direction.

Lupe pulled at my arm. "Leave it alone, Zambia. C'mon."

But Mr. Gore heard me. "The man's just trying to make a living, Arzalia. You're always knocking him. He's a businessman. People want stuff, he gets it for 'em. It's the law of supply and demand. Plus, he takes care of his family, and he gives money to the church."

"Correction. Snake's not raising all his family," I heard Uncle Lamar say. "Not with us having to raise Zambia."

Say what? When I jerked around toward him, my

pecan pie almost slid off my plate. "So what did he mean by that?" I whispered to Lupe.

"Nothing, Zambia," Lupe said. "He was just talking. Ease up."

"You sure? Didn't sound like 'nothing' to me. But if you say so." I set my piece of pie down on the table with all the meat loaf and chicken. I wasn't hungry for it anymore.

"Leon, no self-respecting preacher takes money from a drug dealer," Miz Arzalia said. "But like the song says, God's gonna raise up a nation that will obey someday, and the preachers are gonna be the first to feel the pain."

"Don't blame it all on the preachers," Mr. Gore said. "I don't buy anything but beer and cigarettes from Snake, my kids don't take dope and it doesn't come into my house. So it's none of my business what he does. Shouldn't be any of yours either."

Miz Arzalia reared back in her chair and stared at him. Then she stood up. Things got quiet around the meat loaf table. "It ought to be your business," she said. "You don't know *what* your kids are doing. You don't even know what Potsey had for lunch today."

Mr. Gore opened his mouth, then closed it. "Which *ain't* any of your business either," he said. "Now what else about Potsey?"

Lupe took me by my arm and tugged. "Let's move. Daddy will fight over Potsey. He's liable to pop Miz Arzalia clear across the yard."

"Yeah, but I bet she'll pop him back too," said Aretha, who liked Miz Arzalia.

Aunt Limo walked in between them, making time-out signals with her hands. "All right, case closed. Change the subject. Leon, come get yourself some more ribs. Arzalia, try some macaroni and cheese."

"Go ahead, Aunt Limo!" I said. "Told them, didn't she? Aunt Limo always knows how to keep the peace." I caught her eye and smiled a little at her. Lupe, Aretha, and I returned to the streetlight. Women and men walked in and out of the Paradise, laughing, hollering loudly, waving, passing cigarettes back and forth. Just then I saw Potsey walk past the Paradise with some guy. I recognized his big chest and muscular arms under one of those thin-strap T-shirts he loved to wear. I bumped Lupe. "Look! Potsey! Did you know he was gonna be over here?"

"You know Potsey goes where he wants to go."

Potsey didn't see me. Too bad. I fanned myself with my hat while my eyes followed his ponytail bobbing away through the crowd. I thought I saw the earring in his right ear sparkle at me though.

Potsey—well, his real name was Eduardo, but nobody called him that—was into weight lifting. He called himself an Afro-Hispanic and used to say that after he finished high school he was going to be the world's first professional Afro-Hispanic weight lifter. Potsey stopped saying that after he was suspended from sixth grade for three months last spring—because he'd brought a falling-to-pieces, rusty machete to gym class. He said he did it because other kids had brought their knife collections to school and gave reports, and he wanted to do it too. He hardly ever went to school at all anymore. Now kids were bringing guns.

If our pastor, Reverend Stoney Reed, who was also a teacher there, hadn't run down the hallway after Potsey and the cops, the cops would've put Potsey in the police car. We'd have seen Potsey frowning out at us through a police car window on the six o'clock news like he'd been accused of robbing or killing somebody. Rev. Reed taught social studies, was pastor of Temple of Divine Revelations Church, ran a grocery store, and stood up for us kids in school.

Rev. Reed told those cops, "No, you won't take this young man out of school. Call his father first." They did what she said too. Then she bawled out the principal for calling the cops in the first place.

I lost all sight of Potsey when a cable television truck pulled up beside a telephone company truck parked at the club. That tied up traffic even worse. "Uncle Snake must have big-screen TVs in there," Aretha said. "But they're working awfully late, aren't they?"

"Girl, they're not fixing TVs and telephones," said Lupe. "They deliver cocaine in those trucks all over the county. In beer trucks too. Cab drivers and pizza drivers do it too."

I frowned. "And how do you know so much?"

" 'Cause I watch CNN Headline News," Lupe said. " 'Cause Potsey tells me, stupid!"

"Look, look, look!" Aretha squealed. "A fight!"

We crouched down and peeked between the cars. Right in front of the club, these two guys were swinging their fists at each other. Then one guy hopped on the other one. They rolled about on the ground. People crowded around.

"Look out, he's got a knife!" a woman screamed. I leaned around the fender of a car and saw a woman jerk and pull at the man on top of the other one. The men rolled apart and leapt to their feet.

"Mess with me!" The first man swiped at the other one.

"Try to cut me, huh?" The second guy jumped back and jammed his hand inside his shirt. "I'll put a bullet through your brain!"

The crowd fell back. "Stop, Clevonne!" the woman hollered. She struggled with the one called Clevonne, and finally pulled him away from the crowd and the other man.

"Don't come over here no more!" the other man shouted. "And don't bring your raggedy butt to Snake's new place in Deacons Neck, either, else you'll be a dead man."

The woman and Clevonne got into a car double-parked by the club. With a screech of tires the car tore up the street, almost smashing into another car coming toward it.

"Never a dull moment on Garvey Avenue." Lupe stood up. "Did you see a gun? I didn't."

"No, but did you just now hear that man say Snake had something new in Deacons Neck?" I pressed my hat down on my head and spun around.

"Oooh, this is hot," Aretha said. "Daddy and Miz Arzalia'll have heart attacks!" She raced back across the yard with her news.

I puffed out my chest, tipped my hat, and strutted around. My daddy was gonna have *two* nightclubs! "Go ahead, Snake. My daddy's gonna have the wildest, baddest, hottest, loudest, jumpingest club in Deacons Neck!"

Lupe laughed. "Oh, that old cat was just drunk."

"Maybe, maybe not. But guess what, Lupe. What if it is true?" I tapped her on the head with my hat. "If I work it right, maybe I can get a gig there too."

"Sure. C'mon, I wanna hear Aretha's version."

Just as we reached the lodge and caught up with Aretha, we heard a loud screech of car tires and *Bam! Bam! Bam! Bam! Bam! Bam! Bam!*

Lupe screamed. Aretha and I scrambled to the landing and squatted down under the steps, with Lupe pushing in behind us.

Pop! Pop! Pop! Pop! Pop! Pop! Pop! Pop! Pop! Pop! Pop! Pop! Pop!

Between my fingers I saw Miz Arzalia grab her purse and duck behind a tree. Aunt Limo and Mr. Gore dropped down by a barbecue grill with fish still sizzling in it.

"Oh, now they got to shoot!" a man in the lodge yard yelled. Covering their heads with their arms, people rushed from around the club and scattered up and down the street.

Bam! Bam! Bam! Bam! Bam! Bam! People ran into the street, into the lodge yard, into chairs and tables, into hedges, into each other.

Silence.

I took a deep breath. When a car door somewhere slammed, Aretha jumped.

"Aretha, Zambia, where are you?" Aunt Limo called out.

"Lupe?" Mr. Gore shouted.

"Over here," Aretha squeaked. "We're all okay." I patted the ground for my hat, which had fallen off when Lupe bumped into me. We crawled out from our hiding place.

Snake walked out of the club and stood on the steps under the light, looking around. Then he laughed, making the scar that tunneled from the edge of his right eyebrow down to his lip move up and down his face. I heard that he'd got cut from being slashed with a broken bottle. "Y'all afraid of a few firecrackers?" he hollered. "Happy Fourth of July!"

The gold chains around his neck glittered. He smoothed his hands down the front of his shiny blue shirt, then returned to the club. The jukebox took off again. I saw Uncle Lamar standing in the doorway of the lodge.

Slowly people began to stand back up. They began to appear from around bushes, cars, and houses. "Snake said it was just fireworks, a joke," I whispered to Lupe. "He is so cool. I wasn't scared."

"You lie," Lupe said. "You were so scared your hat got here before you did. *Papacita*'s calling me. *Adiós, amigas.*"

We rushed straight to Uncle Lamar's car and got in. Aunt Limo set half-empty cake plates and macaroni pans inside the trunk just any old way.

"Sis, Retha, you all in?" Uncle Lamar tried to start up his car. "Firecrackers, huh. I know what an AK-47 rifle being fired sounds like. I called the police, but they're not here yet. Come on, car, let's go now."

Other lodge folks were snatching and pulling to get their tablecloths, silverware, and themselves out of there too. Uncle Lamar pumped the gas pedal hard.

The old Datsun finally jumped forward, and we shot out into the street.

"I'm gonna stop by city hall tomorrow," Uncle Lamar told Aunt Limo, "and see if Snake's taken out a club license."

"Can't he open up a club without everybody getting upset?" I couldn't hold it back. "Mr. Gore said he was just trying to be a businessman."

"Not your father's kind of business, honey," Miz Arzalia said. "You don't know your daddy like we do. That crowd he's got at the Paradise in Gumbo Grove will be right over here. Did you know that he pays off the police to let him do his devilment?"

"But—"

"Hush up, Zambia," Aunt Limo broke in. "Lamar, let me talk to Snake."

"I didn't see a single police car tonight," Miz Arzalia went on. "I kept my purse right by me all the time tonight, afraid some hoodlum—"

"Arzalia, let it alone for a while, please," Aunt Limo said.

Everybody got quiet. After a few minutes Uncle Lamar spoke up again. "Remember when a guy tried to open up that beer joint in Bert Green's old garage about ten years back? That guy lasted one month, girls, and gave up because Reverend Reed and her church and all us families got together and closed him down. Place has been boarded up ever since.'' He laughed. ''Remember how we went to the city council meeting and protested? That was one time when the mayor and the police chief listened.''

''Lamar, you can let it alone too,'' Aunt Limo said.

As soon as we got back home, I flopped down on my bed, thinking. ''Aretha, what if I went and lived with Snake and them?''

''Why would you wanna do that?'' Aretha looked at me like I was nuts. ''The Two Stooges don't like you. They didn't even speak to you tonight. You can just keep your little butt right here. I guess I can put up with you some more.''

I sat there thinking. Finally we went to bed.

''Are you mad?'' Aretha whispered from her side of the room. ''You have nightmares if you go to sleep mad.''

''I'm not mad. Just thinking.''

Thinking that if Snake really did open a club over here, maybe he'd want me to help him. Thinking that maybe if I lived with Seritta, I'd know what it was like to really have a sister, and not a cousin around. Most important, I was thinking I could be around my dad.

When I opened my eyes the next morning, Aretha's face hung over mine. ''Yo, sleepyhead. C'mon. It's Saturday, remember? Parade time.''

I sat up. ''Oh, yeah. Nothing else to do over here

today anyway but go to this ole fair. Man, I'd kill to be over on Garvey. I bet that street's gonna pop all weekend."

"You were popping in your sleep too," Aretha said. "Moaning, groaning, and squealing. I told you not to go to bed mad. You must have been having some terrible dreams. Must have been because of all that thinking. Are you mad at me over what I said about Seritta and them?"

"No."

"Good. I didn't mean it, but I think you ought to stay here," she said.

Aretha buzzed Lupe on the phone to get her moving too. Before long we hooked up with Lupe and were headed for downtown Deacons Neck. Which wasn't very far. Nothing in this little old country town was. We passed our church and Reverend Reed's grocery store. It was right by the old garage, the one that she helped to close down when it was a bar.

In school Reverend Reed was always after us to use our problem-solving and thinking skills. She was forever after me to think clearly: *Zambia, think it out.* She'd be telling us to take our time, think it through. Identify the problem. Decide if it really is. List our options, make a decision, put our plan into action, and then evaluate what we did.

Shoot, I didn't have time to do all that! It was okay to do in church and in school, but not anyplace else, where it really mattered.

We passed the garage. The weeds finally had been cut, but it was still junky.

"I'm glad somebody cut that stuff," Aretha said.

"Shoot, getting that grass cut was the most exciting thing to happen on the street this whole holiday weekend," I said. "And we missed it. Silver Dollar Road will always be deader than a cemetery."

A huge white banner hung across Strom Thurmond Highway where it intersected with our street. CALVARY COUNTY INDEPENDENCE DAY FAIR it read, with a big red firecracker flapping at each end.

"I hope somebody's selling good lemonade this year," I said. "Last year's tasted like dishwater."

"Don't count on it," Aretha told me. "This is still the same old rinky-dink square dancing, hog calling, pig wrestling, tricycle racing, baby kissing county fair that they've been having for the last fifty years."

"You left out the teen dances in the co-op tent," I reminded her. "We can't miss those, girl."

"And dance to 'Shag Forever' played by the Wacawachee Cottonball Stump Band," Lupe screamed. "Or hear that same old sad rap group from Blue Swamp, and dance with those same ole turnip head–looking dudes from Lansboro. You know the ones I mean. Last year they spit lemonade seeds at each other. Give me a break."

"Well, I'm thrilled, because otherwise I'd be scraping dirt out the corners of the kitchen floor," I said. "Or scrubbing and digging and wringing out the mop, just like I was in prison."

Aretha frowned at me, but I didn't care. I bet I wouldn't have to do it if I lived with Snake.

In the town square the Confederate flag flapped

over the statue of the Confederate soldier like a big red-and-blue bird. First Baptist Church's bell rang out the hour. On Ninth Avenue, our main drag, we passed racks of clothes and tables of dishes, pots, and pans leaning in front of the stores. American flags, South Carolina and Confederate flags snapped and rippled everywhere. Two white-haired saleswomen watched us through the windows of Bardee's Variety Store like they thought we were going to steal an eggbeater. Lupe and I lingered around the table for an extra few seconds, staring back at them, then went on.

"At least if we were on the beach we could go into the beachwear stores and look at the T-shirts," said Lupe.

We headed for the post office to sit on the steps for the parade. Large green-and-white striped tents, gray bleachers, and tan National Guard tents stood on the soccer field behind the high school.

Just as we reached the corner, Seritta and Meritta, in Snake's minivan, stopped in front of the Wet 'N Dry Wholesale Liquor Store. Talk about luck! When I saw Seritta and Meritta look over at us, I put on my special smile again. Maybe they just didn't see me last night.

Seritta leaned out the window. "Hey, Zambia, what's happening?"

I was so surprised, I almost forgot to speak. "Hey! What're you doing over here?"

"Slumming," she said. "No, I'm joking. We came over for the parade. Say, I got something for you. Meet me at—let's see—by the co-op tent this afternoon." She started the van.

We watched them drive away. "I didn't hear a thing and I didn't see a thing," Aretha told Lupe. "I must have just dreamed that one of the Two Stooges spoke to Zambia."

I came out of my coma. "Well, I heard her. And she said she was gonna give me something at the dance. You heard her, didn't you, Lupe? Aretha, what'd I say about calling them names? Wonder what's she gonna give me? Money? Clothes?"

"A beating or a dog-doo sandwich, something like that," Aretha said. "If she's gonna give you something, it'll probably be something you don't want to have, like trouble."

"Shut up, Aretha. You always got to think the worst. That's why they don't speak to me half the time—because of your attitude." I snapped my fingers in Aretha's face. She stopped laughing. "In case you forgot, they *are* my sisters. Give them some respect."

"My attitude?" Aretha frowned. "Oh, excuse me, but neither me or my attitude want to be around your . . . *sis*tuhs. And from the way they treated you last night, they don't want to be around you either."

"Maybe if you were polite, they'd speak more. You and Uncle Lamar just like to bad-mouth people." I jabbed my finger at her. "You didn't even speak to them just now."

"They didn't speak to me either! Lupe, she's gone crazy!" Aretha pecked Lupe on the shoulder. "She told me last night she wanted to go live with them. Girl, you just do what you want with your ole *sis*tuhs. Go live with them. I need my own room."

"Then I could do whatever I wanted and get whatever I liked, and I wouldn't have to be in your ole funky room, or—"

"You all chill," Lupe broke in. "Aretha, quit calling people names. Zambia, you're not moving anywhere. Make up now and be cool. I told you all you didn't know how to act in public."

I stamped on ahead to the post office and found a seat on the steps. Lupe sat down beside me. Aretha sat down by herself. "I thought you were going to go to blows. What's up?"

"Lupe, see, it's like I wish I had my own family. You and Aretha got your own dads right there with you. I don't. I don't have my momma either. You all do."

"But you got your uncle Lamar and aunt Limo. They're your family." She shrugged. "You're right. I can't talk about how you feel. But I do know that the way you think and talk is gonna put your behind in a sling one of these days, and probably mine too."

C • H • A • P • T • E • R

3

Police Chief Katz, in his big white car with the dome on top spinning bright blue lights, rolled toward us. He was followed by the Deacons Neck High School ROTC color guard, the mayor in a little red convertible, and then a bunch of other big-time folks.

I saw Aunt Limo poke her head out the door of the Twilight Motel next door and look over at Aretha sitting by herself. Then she saw me. Then I saw all of her come out of the motel through the doorway and bounce across the street to Aretha. Next thing I knew she was right by me.

"I bet you think Aretha and me had a fight, huh," I said before she could get started.

"Keep on talking," was all she said.

"Well, it wasn't my fault. It was like this . . ."

She listened. When I had finished, she wiped her face with a paper napkin, then fanned herself. "So what else is new? You've been pecking at each other since you were babies. Right after you turned four and came to live with us, Aretha tried to get bossy. When you cussed her out instead, she hit you in the head with her milk cup. The next day you ate her candy bar and then walked right around with her for two hours afterward, pretending to help her look for it."

I thought the candy trick was pretty funny, but not the milk cup part, and said so.

"My sister—your aunt Canolia—used to tie me up with my own jump rope and keep me at the table until I ate my black-eyed peas," Aunt Limo said. "Just because she heard Momma say I had to eat them. I hate black-eyed peas to this day, but Canolia and I get along now."

"Aretha and I aren't sisters, just cousins. I got two half sisters and they've never hit me."

Aunt Limo waved the napkin at me. "Cousins, sisters, it doesn't matter in the long run, Miss Hardhead. We're still family, and we are blessed. So get along. Kids fight. Case closed."

I took a chance. "Aunt Limo, Seritta wants to meet me at the dance this afternoon. She said she had something for me."

"Like what?"

"I don't know. Won't be poison or trouble, I know that."

"Good, 'cause Seritta's the one who likes to play little tricks on you, isn't she? Or is it Meritta?" Aunt Limo looked at me real sharp.

"What tricks?" Did she know about the time Meritta pushed me into the broom closet at the mall in Gumbo Grove and locked me in? Seritta had to find a security guard to get me out.

"Go ahead." She smiled a little. "Just use your common sense before you do anything. Seritta's a nice kid, but she's getting a bad reputation. You'd walk off a cliff if she told you to."

"I would not." I stared at a tractor rolling by, decorated with balloons and red, white, and blue ribbons, while I tried to think of some things to tell Aunt Limo to prove that I knew how to think and act. I couldn't come up with anything big. "I can think good. Reverend Reed said so," I said instead.

"How's my girl?" said a voice beside me. When I looked around, I saw that it was old Mr. Shinshiner, one of our neighbors. His daughter was pushing him in his wheelchair. He sat on his front porch almost every day playing his radio-TV. Sometimes he had me bring him bread from Reed's grocery store. He was the only white person on our block and had been there forever, I guess. A little truck brought him hot lunch and dinner every day. I went to school with his granddaughter.

"Hey, Mr. Shinshiner. Need anything from the store?" I asked.

Mr. Shinshiner smiled, showing his false teeth. "No, I got my chauffeur to handle things today," he said, patting his daughter's hand.

We turned back to the parade. Aunt Limo pointed. "Now, is that too bold or what?"

Driving up the street in the parade was Snake, in his minivan, pulling a pink-and-black crepe-paper-swirled float! In glittery silver letters across the front of the float was SNAKE'S PARADISE NUMBER 2, DEACONS NECK, S.C.

On the float Seritta, Meritta, Potsey, and some other kids from Deacons Neck waved and danced to loud,

loud rap music. They wore pink and black Paradise Number Two T-shirts and visors.

"Look! Look at Snake!" I was jumping and waving. "Snake! Hey, Snake!" And guess what? He saw me! Seritta did too. They both waved at me. "Hey, Potsey!"

"Here, Zambia! Hey, Miss Limo!" Snake threw visors at us. I caught mine and jammed it on my head. Aunt Limo's fell in the dust. She picked it up. I left her staring at her cap to rush over to Lupe.

"Did you see that fabulous float? Did you see Potsey? Girl, my daddy's rich, rich, rich! He does have a new place over here. And look!" I touched my visor. "Aunt Limo said I could go see Seritta too. How could she say no? Lupe, my luck is changing at last!"

"What I saw was Potsey. And what I predict is that Momma's gonna have a fit about it." Lupe had a funny look on her face. "So you're gonna see Seritta. Wow. Don't act like it's a big deal when you get around her, 'cause it's not and she's not either. Act like you got some sense. You won't know what she wants until after she tells you, anyway."

"How come she's gotta be wanting something? She said she was gonna give me something."

"'Cause that's how people do," Lupe said. She waved at kids who threw us candy as they rolled by on fire trucks.

"You sound like Aunt Limo. I know what I'm doing. You're just jealous 'cause Potsey was on the float and you weren't."

"So? You weren't either," she shot back.

I shut up. She had a point there. I didn't pay much

attention to the rest of the parade, except for the three pigs that trotted past with their straw hats hanging every which way around their necks.

I touched my visor every ten seconds. What if Seritta gave me something really fantastic, like a suitcase full of new clothes? What if she and Snake took me to Epcot Center? What if she asked me to come live with them?

"Hello in there. Are you still on the planet with us?" Lupe waved her hand in front of my face. "The parade's ended. Let's go watch the bungee jumpers."

A crane sat in the middle of the soccer field. High in the air, hanging off the crane, was a bungee platform with a couple of people standing on it. Down on the ground, looking like a humongous raft, was the landing pad. We joined a big crowd of people standing behind ropes by the raft.

"You know one darn thing," I heard a man say to another man. "Anybody who thinks it's fun to jump out of an Easter basket a million feet in the air and bounce up and down by a rubber band wrapped around his legs has got to have the brains of a bird."

"Yeah, but at least a bird can fly," the other man said.

Suddenly the gate of the little platform opened, and giving out a bloodcurdling shriek, a man shot headfirst down through the air toward the ground. Lupe and I screamed and grabbed each other. Just when I was sure this fool was gonna end up a grease spot on the soccer field, he shot back up in the air like a yo-yo.

Everybody yelled and clapped. Finally the man

stopped springing, and they lowered him to the ground. The man stood up and waved his fists in the air. I noticed that the back of his pants were wet.

Lupe looked at her watch. "Let's go find some of that awful lemonade, then go to the dance. It's hot out here."

After walking around a crowd of girl dancers in long black-and-white polka-dot dresses practicing their clogging routine in the middle of the street, we reached the co-op tent. The Wacawachee Cottonball Stump Band was tuning up instruments at one end. At the other end, by the refreshment tables, a couple of zit-faced boys threw ice at each other. One of the boys nudged the other one . . . and started walking toward us. One dude wore a New York Knicks cap high on his long head. The other guy had one thick dreadlock hanging down from the top of his otherwise bald head, which sat at the top of a long, skinny neck. They both wore dark sunglasses, military boots, white T-shirts, and army pants.

"Beavis and Butthead!" Lupe said. I burst into giggles and turned toward the door, but before Lupe could follow, the first boy stepped in front of her.

That's when I saw Seritta outside the tent through a flap in the wall. I forgot about Lupe and ran for the exit. "Be cool," I told myself. "Check her out first. No matter what she gives you, be cool." I cleared my throat a couple of times, and adjusted my visor.

I stepped into the blindingly bright July sun and, trying not to trip over the tent ropes, reached Seritta.

"Daddy said to tell you happy birthday and to give

you this card," she said, smiling. "The cap is your birthday present from Daddy, me, and Meritta."

"Oh! Hey, thanks." I took the card. "Okay." And then I didn't know what else to say.

"Well?" Seritta laughed a little, and her light-brown eyes sparkled.

"Yeah, right on. Hey, tell, tell—uh—tell him I said thanks. Thanks for the card." I took the visor off, looked at it, wiped off a speck of dust, and slid it back on my head. "Thanks for this. That was a sharp float too. And is he really gonna open up a place over here?"

She nodded. "Next Wednesday night's the grand opening, with a boss band, free food, a wet T-shirt contest, and a dance contest. We're gonna throw down. Anybody can come. You too. I mean, if Uncle Lamar and Aunt Limousine say so."

"I *know* how to deal with them," I said, wondering how I would. "Where's it gonna be?"

"At Snake's Paradise Number Two, of course," she said.

"Where's that?"

"If you know how to deal with Uncle Lamar, then you should know how to deal with finding out where the club is." Seritta winked at me and swished away.

I quickly opened the envelope and pulled out the card. There was a picture of a yellow flower and the words *Happy Birthday* on the front of the card, and inside—a $20 bill! I grabbed that bill quick. Money from my father! First time! Check me out, the birthday girl! Didn't matter that he was six weeks late. Better late than never. I stuffed the bill in my money belt, eyeing people as they passed, wanting to tell them the great news about what my daddy just gave me. My daddy, Snake LaRange.

But then I thought, "Whoa!" If I told even Lupe and Aretha, they might want to borrow some, or make me buy them something. Not that I was selfish, you know, but this was special money, coming from my dad, and I wanted to spend it in special ways, on myself. I decided not to tell anybody.

Lupe found me at the hot dog stand, holding a footlong hot dog with chili, onions, ketchup, lettuce, and mustard in one hand, a cup of lemonade in the other, and a bag of potato chips under my arm.

"Where'd you get all that food? Can I have a bite, please?" She sucked on the lemonade, then nibbled at my hot dog. "*Gracias*. Whew! Finally got away from that *boy!*" Giggling, she curved her fingers into claws. "Dig this, ZamBee: He asks me if I want some lemonade, so I'm like, sure, 'cause then I won't have to spend my little *centavos*." She stopped to take a pull at my lemonade. "But when I say okay, he tells me to go ahead and buy it—and buy one for him, 'cause he's thirsty too—and I'm supposed to pay for it all!"

I almost dropped my potato chips on that one. "Jive turkey," I said. "And you almost fell for it."

"Daggone straight. Now, where'd you get the money for this food?" She kept chewing. "You told me you were broke."

Just then we both saw Aretha. She saw us, too, and came over. "Where'd you get the hot dog?"

"At the hot dog stand," I said, taking another bite.

Aretha watched me. "Aren't you gonna offer me a bite?"

"Here, girl. You can have the rest." 'Course, there wasn't much left.

"Thanks."

When Lupe told Aretha about the boy's trick, Aretha laughed. Then she looked at me and got serious. "Uh, Zambia, you still gonna meet Seritta at the tent?"

"I already did."

"Oh." She glanced at Lupe. "Oh. I thought we were all going over there. Together. So, what happened?"

I opened my bag of potato chips, taking my time. "Not much."

For a long minute nobody said anything. Lupe raised her shoulders and hands in the air. "So what'd she give you?"

"A birthday card," I said, "and a message from Snake. My father."

"What was it?" Aretha put in.

"What was what?"

Lupe sighed. "The message, ZamBee."

"None ya." I winked at her like Seritta had.

Aretha let out a sigh too. "None ya what?"

"None ya business," I said back. "Can you deal with that? If you can, then you can deal with finding out." I tried to laugh like Seritta did.

"Five minutes with Seritta and the girl trips out," Lupe told Aretha.

The three of us wandered around the fair, nobody saying much to each other. I know I should have told them everything, since they always told me everything, but right now I liked having a secret just between me, Seritta, and Snake.

I saw Seritta coming straight toward me with two girls who'd been on the float.

"Zambia, don't forget about the party." Seritta snapped her fingers at me.

"I can deal with that!" I said.

"What party? Where? When?" said Lupe. "Zambia, c'mon now! I told you about the barbecue, remember?"

"Nobody's heard about this party but them, I guess," Aretha said. "Must be by special invitation."

I kept quiet, hoping they'd beg.

Aretha twisted her mouth at me. "She doesn't want to say, Lupe, 'cause I'm here. She thinks I'll tell Momma. You keep your ole party to yourself, Zambia. I don't care." She stamped off to the dance tent.

I opened my mouth to say something back, but Lupe shook her finger at me. "Ease up, Sister Too-Tough. You keep firing at us, we're gonna fire back, and somebody's feelings are gonna get hurt bad. Sure enough won't be mine."

"Won't be mine either." I studied my Nikes, then bent down and dusted off the right toe. "Aretha's jealous 'cause I'm getting some play from Seritta."

"No, she's not, Zambia, and you know it. Nobody cares but you. Seritta's your sister, but she's no big deal. You talk stupid sometimes."

I took a step back. "She's a big deal to me."

Lupe just shook her head. "What did Seritta give you—some ignorant pills?"

"Look. See? She gave me a birthday card from Snake, with twenty dollars." I pulled the card and money out of my belt. "I bet Snake's been wanting to give me stuff all the time and Uncle Lamar wouldn't let him."

"A little twenty-dollar bill? Umph, umph, umph." Lupe shook her head again. "With all the money your father has, he shoulda been giving you hundreds of dollars all the time. A thousand, even. I mean, he coulda been buying you clothes and everything. Coulda bought you a new house."

"But—"

"So but nothing," Lupe snapped. "Shut up."

I closed my mouth.

"And give your uncle some credit for feeding your silly behind all these years."

"Wait a minute. Don't tell me to shut up." I put my hands on my hips. "I got a right to say something too."

"Not if it's gonna be dumb."

"Okay, Uncle Lamar's all right. I just want it better. Maybe Snake has a bank account set up for me. Maybe he has me in his will. Maybe—"

Lupe snapped her fingers in my face. "Zambia, he only gave you a fifty-cent hat and twenty dollars. You act like it's a million dollars. Get real!"

I looked away. For once Lupe didn't understand. Maybe Potsey would. He and his dad were close.

Lupe nudged me with her elbow. "Plus, where's *my* visor?"

"Now I know why you're so mad! You don't have a cap." I snatched my visor off and slid it on her head, glad to change the subject. "You can wear it for five minutes. Now will you ease up on *me*?"

"Okay, if you tell me about this party. Where is it, what time is it, and what are *we* gonna wear?"

"It'll be at the new Paradise Number Two." We started walking again. "But she didn't exactly say anything about me inviting other people."

"Zambia, if she invited you, she's already invited everybody else. And where exactly *is* this Paradise Number Two?"

I hesitated. When I said I didn't know, Lupe waved me off and walked away.

C • H • A • P • T • E • R

4

By the sound of the accordion music, I recognized the Wacawachee Cottonball Stump Band, crucifying another song. I started to follow Lupe to the co-op tent to see what Aretha was up to. But just then I noticed Seritta and Meritta waving at me. They were on the lot by Snake's float.

I ran right over too. "I got something to eat with that money Snake gave me," I said.

"What'd you get?" Meritta pulled on one of her fake curls. "Chitlins?"

"Stop, Meritta," Seritta said. "ZamBee, would you like a ride over to Uncle Lamar's? We gotta go over to Silver Dollar Road."

"In the van?" I asked. I tried to keep my mouth from hanging open, like Lupe had warned.

"No, we're gonna drag you behind it on a rope," Meritta said.

I cut my eyes at her. "I'm talking about like not riding back on the float, girl. Sure, Seritta, I can deal with that."

Seritta pulled open the side door and I hopped in. I couldn't help but rub my hand over the thick blue shag carpeting on the walls and floor. I plopped down on one of the blue-and-white velvety pillows. A drum rhythm thudded softly through the walls. Two light-skinned dancers shook their sugar in a video playing on a big-screen TV bolted to a wall. A brown box sat by another wall. Seritta slid into the driver's seat. Meritta climbed into the back with me.

I bit my lips to make sure that they weren't hanging. When I felt Meritta's eyes on me, I settled back against the wall like where I was wasn't any big deal. But inside I was shouting. This was some Saturday, turning out boss after all!

"Bet you've never been in a van like this, huh?" she said.

When I shook my head, she added, "I knew you hadn't, not in ole dead Deacons Neck. Want a Coke? Or a beer?" She reached over to the brown box. A refrigerator!

"C-C-Coke."

Meritta handed me a can. She pulled out a beer from the refrigerator, popped the lid, and lifted the can toward me. "Sure? Okay, it's gone." She took a long pull of beer, smiled, wiped her lips, then poured some into a plastic cup and handed the cup up front to Seritta.

We drove off, music thumping and vibrating through me. This was some smooth riding. No rackety-clacks or pops, pings, and backfirings either. I pressed my face against the tinted glass and stared out at the people and cars we passed, knowing nobody could see in. But wouldn't it have been sharper if they could have seen me? They'd be saying, "Whoa, there goes Snake's girls!"

"So, when you get through slobbering up the window," said Meritta, "tell me what you do over at Uncle Lamar's besides scrub floors and watch TV."

Meritta was starting to get on my nerves, for true! I slid back down toward the pillow, missed it, and landed on the floor. I shifted around to make her think I'd planned to do that. "Nothing. It's a bore."

"I guess so, with Aretha there. Ole Cuz is too dull and too dumb." Meritta waved her hand at me. "I am *too* tired of her. I know you have absolutely got to be, huh?"

Meritta, I said inside, *you* are too tired too. I was surprised to realize that I didn't dig what she said about Aretha either. "Thanks for the Coke," I said instead. "It's sure better than that nasty lemonade."

"Did you find out where our party's gonna be?" Seritta asked from the front.

I started to lie, but changed my mind. "Not yet. Are you gonna send out invitations?"

"Invitations . . . oh, no!" Meritta burst out laughing. "Yeah, like how they say to do in *Good Housekeeping.*"

"Well, but Snake is rich. That's how rich folks do," I snapped.

"Zambia's right," Seritta told Meritta. Seritta looked at me through her rearview mirror. "Daddy did send some letters out to the funeral home director, some ministers, the police chief, folks like that. I know 'cause I delivered them."

"So? Well. Hmmm." Meritta shrugged. "But he wouldn't give one to *her*. I mean, not to kids."

"Why not?" Seritta shot back. "He gave one to you."

"Forget I said anything," Meritta said.

Thanks, Seritta, I said inside. I found the pillow. Look at Snake's girls, riding in style now! I snapped my fingers to a song, and started to hum. That song got so good to me that I had to mouth the words. Meritta raised her eyebrows. "You do that pretty good," she said.

"Thanks." My cheeks got hot. A compliment, finally, from her?

"Maybe next time you can learn how to say words out loud," Meritta added. I cut my eyes at her. "It's a joke, Zambia," she said.

When the next song came on, Meritta started to sing. "C'mon, do it with me," she said to me.

By the time we pulled up to Uncle Lamar's house, Meritta, Seritta, and I were all singing. I stopped, though, when I saw Aretha and Lupe turn the corner onto our block. Reverend Reed's car sat in our driveway. I bet she was organizing another church revival. She held them all the time.

Meritta pulled out a tube of lipstick from her leather bag and spread it thick on her lips. Then she went to work with eyeliner and powder. "You need to have a makeup session, honey," she said. "You don't even wear your lipstick right. Or is that Popsicle juice?"

"Go suck on a prune," I said.

Meritta blinked.

Seritta screamed out a laugh. "Score one for Zambia," she said. "Serves you right, Meritta. You tease too much."

I climbed out of the van after Seritta opened the door. "Next time I'll have to teach you how to wear makeup." Meritta climbed out after me. "Serious, I will. You're all right."

"This was hip, dynamite," I said to Seritta. "Oh, and tell, uh, Snake, I mean, uh—"

"Say Daddy, or Snake, or go back to whatever you been calling him, Zambia," said Seritta. "With all this stuttering you sound like you got some sort of defect with your mouth."

"Yeah, tell Snake I said thanks again."

Seritta nodded, got back in the van, and drove away. Lupe and Aretha, who I knew must have seen everything, marched past me without saying a word and into the house.

When I reached the porch, I heard Aunt Limo's fast, high-pitched fussing. Then, through the screen door, I saw her bang her tiny fist into her palm. "I'm so tired of people coming to me about Snake!"

"The city told me that Snake bought Bert Green's old garage two months ago," Uncle Lamar was saying. "He's had since May to fix it up. Now, Bert is a policeman—he knows Snake! Why'd he sell him his lot?"

Aha! I told myself. The old garage—right across from Lupe's house—was only seven or eight houses up the street from me! I saw the minivan parked up the street in front of the garage. There was Snake's Jeep too. So there it was, Snake's new Paradise Number Two!

"Yes!" Grinning, I doubled up my fist and jerked my bent arm down to my side. And then I listened some more.

"He's got all the licenses he needs." Uncle Lamar was still talking. "So there's nothing we can do about that part either."

"Well, we ought to see what sort of clientele he brings in," Aunt Limo said. "He could be trying to finally establish a legitimate, honest business over here. Maybe he wants to settle down away from the beach and all that crime."

"Snake never has done anything honest except get born," Rev. Reed said. "You know that."

"Excuse me," Aunt Limo snapped, "but this is my brother you're talking about."

"Better yours than mine," Rev. Reed said back. "Two Sundays ago when you didn't make it to church Snake showed up. He almost preached a sermon during testimonials about how he wanted to help our community. Then he tried to put a hundred dollars into my collection plate, but I wouldn't let him. I heard he went around talking to our neighbors and giving them money too."

"Talking to the neighbors?" Uncle Lamar grunted. "He sure didn't talk to me. You mean he lied to the neighbors. I wonder if he talked to the police too."

"Probably. He hired off-duty policemen to be his security guards over in Gumbo Grove," said Rev. Reed.

I sat down in the porch swing, still listening. Snake

was smart! He had thought everything out. He had a plan! I hoped I could get to be smart like him too.

"What are we going to do?" I heard Uncle Lamar say. "All those trashy people he has around him'll be hanging out on our sidewalks again, selling cocaine, cussing and drinking, breaking into our houses and cars. What about the girls here? Some guy might try to rape them. Can't you preachers get together and stop this madness?"

"I mentioned it to some of the preachers and they said . . . well, they . . . Lamar, they said if Snake had put money into *their* collection plates, it would have stayed there."

I heard a chair squeak. "I'm gonna go talk to the neighbors too," Uncle Lamar said. "We didn't get this street straightened up before just to let it go back downhill."

Uncle Lamar came out to the porch with his face screwed up, but he tried to smile when he saw me. "Have fun at the fair, sis?" he asked. Without waiting for my answer, he walked up the street. Rev. Reed came out next.

"Hi, ZamBee, with your pretty self," she said. "Staying smart?"

"You got that right. I'm gonna be as smart as Snake one of these days. Is that old garage really gonna be his nightclub?"

"Perhaps. But it may not be the place where you'll want to be," she said.

"If my father says I can be there, I will." I raised my

chin and folded my arms. "Nobody can keep me off his property if he says I can be on it."

Rev. Reed smiled. "So I guess I'd better be careful what I say about him, else you'll beat me up, right?"

"Naw, I'll let you slide." I grinned at her. "At least you don't dog him like Uncle Lamar and Miz Arzalia do."

Rev. Reed patted me on the arm. "I try not to 'dog' anybody. Take care, honey."

After I got inside I went straight to my room. Aretha and Lupe were watching television. I flopped down on my bed and turned on my radio. The same song that was on in the van jumped out. I sang along again.

"We're trying to watch TV," Aretha said. "Could you turn the radio down?"

"So, watch TV. I got a right to be in here too." I kept rapping. "Unless you don't want me in here."

Lupe stood up. "Here we go again. You *señoritas* call me when you've quit fighting. *Adiós, muchachas.*"

When Lupe headed out the door, Aretha jumped up and followed her. I stayed where I was and sang my song. But when Aunt Limo came to the room and pointed her finger at me, I snapped off the radio and shut up. Aretha returned a few minutes later. She sat on her bed and watched TV again. I was dying to tell Aretha what I'd been doing with Seritta and Meritta. Instead I rolled the radio volume up and down a couple of times to get her attention, but she wouldn't even look over at me or holler. A good ten minutes must have passed without either one of us talking.

"Won't be long before I'll probably be leaving

here," I finally said. I lay back on my bed and crossed my legs. "I rode in the van with Seritta and Meritta. It is so sharp in there. Big ole TV and a real refrigerator are in it. Meritta's gonna show me how to do makeup. I'm gonna be Miss One. Check that out." Aretha picked up a magazine. She couldn't have been reading, though, not after what I'd just said. But she still didn't say anything. "I'll miss you all a lot, but I'll come visit now and then, okay?" I said.

She didn't say a word. I tried to think of something else to say to make her respond, but my brain hit a blank. I stopped swinging my leg. Maybe she didn't even care. "Of course, I'm not going any time real, *real* soon. We gotta get everything straightened out first, you know."

Aretha mumbled something.

I sat up quick. "What?"

"I said I'm sorry you don't like living here anymore," she said. "And I hope you clean up your side of your room better with them than you do with me. That's all."

"It's clean over here." I told myself inside to sweep under my bed first thing in the morning.

I also needed to clean the mirror and straighten the picture of Momma stuck there sideways. The picture was a fuzzy little Polaroid that Uncle Lamar had taken just before Momma went into the hospital down in Charleston. In the picture Momma is sitting on a bed with her hair all over her head in an old-time Afro. Her face is real thin, but she has this huge smile. She'd written in ballpoint pen across the bottom, "ZamBee, this smile be just for you. Luv, Mom."

We didn't get down to Charleston much anymore. The hospital wouldn't let me in anyway because I was too young. I kind of liked to think about her the way she looked in the picture, smiling, just for me.

Thinking about her right now, though, made me sad.

I walked out to the front porch. I sure thought Aretha'd say more than what she had. Maybe she was too surprised to argue. Or maybe she was really sorry. Why'd I try to make her think I was leaving? I guess I'd have to get Sissy's permission too. And what would Aunt Limo and Uncle Lamar do? I hadn't even thought about them. I bet they'd both have fits. Uncle Lamar would say something like, "You can't go. I haven't got you raised up right yet."

Ole dull Silver Dollar Road was even duller on a holiday Saturday, even with a fair going on. The big square-dance contest was going on now. It was so quiet I could hear Miz Arzalia's hens clucking. I plunked down in the swing. I could see Lupe still walking toward home. She must have stopped somewhere. I hoped she wasn't mad at me for leaving her at the fair. I didn't want to lose her as my best friend. I also wanted her to go with me to the grand opening party. No way I'd have the guts to go alone.

I hopped over to the sidewalk and cupped my hands around my mouth. "Lupe!" I hollered, but she didn't turn around. I decided to call her in a couple days. By then she might be calmed down enough to talk.

■

Tuesday morning I woke up with bright sun in my eyes, rotten fish stink from the garbage trucks outside snatching at my nose, and Aunt Limo in the doorway telling me and Aretha what all we had to clean. Finally she left for work at the motels. I went back to sleep.

When I woke up again, my brain had to remind me of the work waiting: wash the dishes, scrub the kitchen floor, and wash and dry the clothes. I couldn't call the twenty-five dollars a week I got from Uncle Lamar an allowance. It was like a tip. Aretha, who got the same amount, acted like it was big money.

With twenty-five dollars a week I couldn't even buy one piece of any clothes Seritta wore. Having my own credit card was a sure-nuff dream. Meritta had a whole pile of them in her purse in the van. I bet Seritta didn't have to wash clothes. And I bet Meritta didn't wash dishes. I bet Sissy didn't do anything but order maids around her house.

Going to the closet, I pulled out our baskets of dirty clothes. Aretha's balled-up socks rolled everywhere. This wasn't even regular wash day. Wednesday was. Aunt Limo must have had a lot on her mind.

"Jeeze, girl, you could have pulled your funky socks apart." I slid the basket across the floor and it hit Aretha's bed.

"What? Huh?" Aretha rolled over and gawked at me with one eye.

I pulled out one of her crumpled-up T-shirts hanging over the basket's side and dropped it on her head. "And you could turn your T-shirts right side in for a change too. You know clothes don't get clean washed wrong side out."

Aretha snatched the shirt from her face and sat up. "Okay, I'm tired of this. Keep it up and I'm gonna smack you."

"Oh, you are?" Remembering the warning Lupe had given me about Aretha firing back, I stepped back.

"You're being nasty for nothing again. You better go on and do what Momma said and leave me alone, else I'll tell Momma about this party you're trying to get to."

I picked up my basket and backed out the door quick. Talk about someone being mad this morning. In the storage room I dropped the basket on the floor and stuffed clothes in the washing machine.

After I got the first load in, I rummaged through the refrigerator, found a couple of doughnuts, and escaped into the hot July morning. I needed one of Rev. Reed's Mountain Dews. I headed up the street for her store, chewing.

Two men stood at the old garage, painting the side wall bright yellow. Another guy raked the weedy parking lot. A large neon sign that spelled out SNAKE'S PARADISE NUMBER TWO in glass curlicues leaned against a nearby tree. Snake's Jeep was parked at the side of the building.

Just as I came up to the garage, Snake himself walked out of it. He held a broken pair of kitchen chairs away from his shiny black baggy pants and shirt.

Gold chains bounced against his chest. One chain held a tiny gold snake charm.

I wiggled my fingers at him shyly, but I guess he didn't see me. He threw the chairs onto the pile of debris that the man had raked. Gathering up my courage, I walked into the parking lot and stood nearby, waiting to get a chance to try again.

"Get this cleaned up now," Snake told the man. "When I said I'd pay you by the hour, that didn't mean you were supposed to lean on this rake in the same spot all day."

When the man said something back, Snake perched a big fist on each side of his hips. "Oh? You must think I'm a fool. What? Shuh, you might not get paid at all."

"You haven't paid me for the other job," the man said, and threw down the rake.

Like two tomcats, Snake and the man circled each other real slow. I backed up. Snake picked up the rake, and began swinging the wood handle at the man hard and fast. The rake head and its long tines swished through the air like steel claws, slicing the air not two inches from my arm. I jumped back.

"Hey, man, ease up!" The man hollered, ducking and dodging the rake handle.

Leaping forward, Snake smacked the man across his face. Blood spurted from the man's nose. "Ease up on that!"

Moaning, holding his bleeding face, the man stumbled up the sidewalk. Snake stood with his back turned to me, leaning on the rake.

"Hello," I said.

Snake whirled around with the rake handle stretched high above his head, ready to strike again. I threw my arms up in front of me.

"Wait, Snake, it's just me, Zambia!"

C·H·A·P·T·E·R

5

Slowly my father bent and lowered the rake to the ground. As he breathed in deep, I let my breath out. Snake drew a handkerchief out of his pocket, and very slowly wiped his face. His scar looked like a hard, red, shiny, angry trail of lava.

"Hey," I said.

He didn't say anything.

"Sorry if I scared you," I said. "I . . . thanks for the birthday present."

Snake stared at me, wiping his hands, frowning, still not speaking. He folded the handkerchief and slipped it into his pants pocket. "Zambia, Zambia," he said, shaking his head. "There are some things you better learn quick about staying alive, else you won't."

My cheeks burned. I bet he thought I was a fool! I thought hard for something hip to say. "Is this really gonna be your club?"

"Did you hear what I just said about staying alive?" he asked.

"Yeah. Is the club over here gonna—"

"Then if you heard what I said, say something to let me know you got some common sense and can understand English, or else get outta here,'' he hissed through his teeth.

I looked down at the ground. He talked like Uncle Lamar did sometimes. What was I supposed to say? ''Okay, I heard you,'' I said, and shrugged.

''That's better. Now, what about my club?''

''I heard you're gonna open another one, that's all.'' I cut my eyes at him. ''The way people've been talking, I'm thinking it's gonna be the slammingest place around.''

''That's what I'm thinking too.'' He raised his eyebrows, nodded once, and finally—at last!—smiled at me. ''At least, it's my plan for it to be. We open Wednesday—yeah, tomorrow night.'' He turned away toward the painters. I got a flash of dollar bills marching one way, and the clothes in the washing machine marching the other.

''Can I help?''

Snake stopped and swung around to me. ''No, I need some real help.''

''I can deal with that,'' I said. ''I can rake.''

''Then knock yourself out. And see those bags of beer cans there? Pull them onto that junk pile. That lumber's gotta go too. Rake it good.''

''Deal. I'll be right back, okay?''

Snake's smile disappeared. ''Naw, naw-naw-naw-naw. If you leave you might not come back, and I'd be waiting all day with this mess still here. Do it now or leave it alone. I don't have time to play games.''

''I only gotta take some clothes out of the—''

''Be working or be gone,'' Snake said. He jerked his

head at me once, his brows raised, and snapped his fingers. Then he stepped back inside the garage.

That left me with the choice of being chewed out by Aunt Limo over the clothes not getting done, or chewed up by Snake and not making any money. Man, what kind of a choice was that? I remembered what Rev. Reed told us in school about this thinking stuff—it wasn't worth diddly-squat.

So it wasn't hard to choose between not making any money and making some. I grabbed up the rake. The rake's teeth tangled in the rough weeds with every pull I made. I had to keep stopping to get them loose. Time was moving fast now. I knew the clothes needed to come out of the washer. Still, there I was, Snake's girl, working for him, making money!

I stopped and posed with the rake for everybody to see me. I also looked around to see if there was anybody close I could holler at. The mail truck rattled by. The driver, Mr. Stackhouse, didn't see me. I saw Mr. Shinshiner on his porch down the street, but I was sure he couldn't see me.

There was Potsey talking into the window of a car from his bicycle. "Hey, Potsey, how you doing?" I waved. Potsey looked up, saw it was me, waved, and went back to his business. That was enough for me.

Rev. Reed, out sweeping the sidewalk in front of her grocery store, saw me, too, but she didn't wave. Miz Arzalia stood by her tall mailbox at the curb, looking at me so hard I had to turn back to raking to get away from her eyes. But I thought about it again. I was just helping my father. What was so wrong with that? I looked over at her again and waved. Then I raked some more.

After a hot, sweaty hour I had raked up a ton of weeds, beer cans, shoes, shingles, newspapers, plastic bags, coat hangers, and paper cups. Two long, spongy, purply blisters had puffed up across both my aching palms. I started for the garage to show my hands to my father, and see if he had any medicine for blisters, but a man trotted into the yard past me, popped into the building, and shut the door in my face.

In a couple of minutes the man and Snake came outside. "Hey, Zambia, when're you gonna be done?" Snake and the man got into the Jeep. "I need to get that mess hauled away *now.*" He started up the engine and, jabbing his forefinger at me, added, "If you wanna help me, you got to move faster than that."

I rushed back to the rake. Was he mad again? "Almost done." The handle stung my hands and my spine felt ready to break, but I refused to let him see me hurting. I'd show Snake what I could do. Uncle Lamar had taught me how to rake right. Me and that rake hit it again. Sweat poured down my face.

"Oh, Zambia!" Snake called. I froze, caught in my downstroke. Had I done something else wrong?

"Good job so far," my father said.

I thought my chest would burst with pride. "No problem." Snake's tape deck blasted out a rap song. He hit the gas pedal in his Jeep and sped away.

But as soon as Snake cut out, I did too. Back at the house, I yanked wet socks and shirts out of the washer and threw them into the drier. Pinching and tugging, I got the rest of the clothes transferred, and tossed another load of dirty ones into the washer.

Trying to leave, I almost ran down Aretha in the hallway. "Momma just called here looking for you," she said as I pushed past her to the outside again. "Hey, what's up?"

"Nothing." I flew down the street toward Snake's. His Jeep hadn't returned yet, thank goodness. When I saw Lupe on her porch, I slowed down a little. Should I tell her my latest good news? Or should I go on by and maybe only nod—just once—with my eyebrows raised, and snap my fingers, the way Snake did?

"I see you over there tearing up that man's yard," Lupe said before I could decide what to do.

"Lupe, I'm making money! I'm working for my dad! Wait'll we get that junk pile hauled away. The place'll really look sharp. We're getting ready for the grand opening."

"Oh, 'we' are?" Lupe laughed. "And how much money are 'we' making?"

I didn't know. "It won't be chump change. Talk to you later."

"Wait!" Lupe hopped off the porch toward me. "If I help you, will you pay me, too, please?"

I saw my money dwindling away. "Pay? No."

Lupe smiled wickedly. "Isn't it you who wants me to go with her to this grand opening? No pay, no Lupe. I guess that means no Zambia either. Now deal with that."

"Oh, man. Cheater. All right, come on."

Back at the nightclub Lupe kicked at a bike tire. "I

never saw all this trash when I walked through here. Where'd this old refrigerator come from? I hope he doesn't expect us to move it too."

When we tried to lift the old bags of beer cans, the rotten bottoms broke open. Which meant that we had to pick up that mess too. That was one *stinky* job, but we got it done.

Lupe pointed at some pieces of plywood on the ground where the bags had sat. "Please, don't let me see any snakes under here."

"With your strong collard-green-fed arms and Arnold Schwarzenegger-size legs, how could you be afraid of a little snake?" I said. I looked around too.

Not only was the wood heavy, but it was also full of rusty nails and crawling with termites. My back still ached. I lifted the wood the way Uncle Lamar showed me—with my leg muscles pushing, too, and that helped. It seemed like it took us forever to move it all, though.

I sat down on a bucket by the garage and examined my hands. Lupe picked at a splinter in her right thumb. "I'm quitting," she said. "Momma's not gonna be too happy about me being over here. When're you getting paid? Where's Snake?"

I wondered where he was too. His Jeep was still gone, and the garage was locked.

Potsey rode up. "Have you all gone into landscaping?" he asked. He stopped and turned up the boom box to full blast.

"Miz Arzalia's gonna get after you," Lupe said to

him over the music. "You know she can't stand loud music."

Potsey leaned back on his bike, and smiled a little. "If Snake can play his music like this in his Jeep, I can do the same on my bike. Miz Arzalia doesn't own the street. I do."

"Whoa!" Lupe and I said together and slapped hands. Which was a mistake, because she hit my blisters, and I hit her thumb.

Snake turned the corner in his Jeep just then. He jerked the Jeep into the yard in a cloud of dust and music. He nodded at us, and went to the painters. They started talking and slapping shoulders and laughing about something. When Snake looked over at Potsey, Potsey immediately punched off his music and began to nod his head in time to Snake's. Snake turned back to the men.

Lupe and I waited for Snake to pay me. "Snake's little chitchat over there is good and fine," said Lupe after a few minutes, "but don't you think you need to get our money?"

I knew I needed to get back to the clothes too. I walked over to where Snake could see me front-on. He kept talking. For a couple of minutes I pretended that I was his partner—you know, Snake and Daughters, Inc., or something. I cleared my throat. He kept talking.

"Well, I'm done," I finally said. "Cleaned up your yard."

Snake looked down at me like he didn't know who I was. Then, as if remembering, he raised his eyebrows and nodded his head once. "Good. Good job. Nice.

Fine.'' He went back to talking with the painters. I stood there some more.

''Zambia, I got to go!'' Lupe hollered. ''When're you gonna get paid?''

I frowned at Lupe. ''I'm coming.''

''Your employee is waiting, man,'' one of the painters said.

Snake looked at me like he was surprised to see me still there. ''Employee? Who? Zambia? So what's up, Zambia?'' he said. ''I'm busy.''

''I thought that maybe, you know, by helping you real good, since you needed it, that you were gonna, well . . .''

''In other words, man, are you gonna give her some cash?'' Potsey said.

''Did I say that I'd pay you?'' Snake said. The scar frowned at me. ''You're the one who grabbed the rake.''

''But . . . but I thought . . .'' I stopped, trying to understand what he meant.

''Keep thinking like that, you're gonna look stupid like this a lot.'' He crossed his arms.

Tears came to my eyes. I stamped over to Lupe.

''Girl, you mean you had me do all this work and he won't pay you?'' Lupe was still loud. ''That man's cold-blooded. I'm going home.''

I followed Lupe, then stopped and glared at Snake, who stood with his arms crossed, watching me.

''I hope nobody gets into that pile and throws it back all over your yard,'' I hollered at him. ''Better watch that pile.''

"Whoa, did she sound on you, Snake!" Potsey laughed.

Snake reached into his pocket. "Zambia," he said, "come get this."

He held up a bill. "Your pay."

"Honey, go get that money," Lupe said.

Talk about relief! I took my time, though, going back. "Here," he said. "I won't bite you." But when I took hold of the bill, he didn't let go of it. "You better learn to open your mouth and say up front what you want. Huh? Say something!"

"Yeah." When he let go of the money, I saw that it was a fifty-dollar bill. I was rich! "Thanks . . . uh . . . Snake. Dad."

"This is a lesson from your ole man to you: Never do a deal unless you know exactly what you're gonna get."

"And when you don't get your deal," Potsey yelled, "then you take 'em out. Right, Snake?"

Snake smiled. "Right. You blow 'em off the map." He went back to the painters.

"Come to me, pesos!" Lupe said when she saw the money. "I get half, right?"

"Half?" I crossed my arms the way my dad did. "Did I say how much I was gonna pay you? Better learn to open your mouth and say up front what you want."

Lupe put her face half an inch from mine. "Just because your daddy's crazy doesn't mean that you can be too. I heard what he told you, but if you do like he says, somebody'll knock your head off! Starting with me. Now give me some money, *Señorita* Hardhead, Too-Tough Brown."

I pulled back. "I was just joking. How about fifteen dollars, 'cause I had to do all that raking before you even came over?" When she nodded, I relaxed.

Lupe went inside her house and brought back two glasses of Kool-Aid. "All that work we did and then Snake acted like he didn't want to pay. Why'd he do his own kid that way?"

"I don't know. I guess he was teaching me a lesson about how to talk straight up with him, and think how he thinks."

"If you say so. But I know that that's how people get killed, fussing over money. I see it on TV all the time." Lupe stood up. "Now, let's go break that bill so I can get my pesos."

Potsey rolled over to us. "How much did you get?" he asked.

"Enough," I said back, smiling at him.

"She got fifty dollars, and she's giving me some," Lupe said.

"I could use some of that too." He swung around and rode over to Snake.

I giggled. "I hope Potsey won't try to take my job," I told Lupe.

Lupe grunted. "Potsey won't do yards, honey. Come on."

Miz Arzalia watched us from her front porch swing. "You girls ought to be careful, going around that place," she said as we went past.

"What place?" I said, slowing down.

"You know *what* place, ZamBee. Honey, I'm only trying to keep you from getting in trouble with your folks. You too, Lupe."

"I'm not in any trouble, and I *been* with my folks," I said to Lupe, but loud enough for Miz Arzalia to hear.

"Yes, ma'am," Lupe told Miz Arzalia. We crossed the street. "Chill out, girl. She knows what she's talking about. Snake gives you a little piece of change again and you act like you're ready to die for him." Lupe poked and pulled on my arm as she talked. "Shoot, I'm gonna start calling you *Señorita* Big Mouth Too-Tough."

"Leave me alone," I told her.

Rev. Reed's store was closed, so we walked to the gas station on Ninth Avenue. When the attendant wouldn't break the bill unless we bought something, we ended up buying potato chips, a six-pack of pop, and candy bars.

"What kind of sense does it make to wash clothes, scrub floors, wash dishes, and do a bunch of other stuff and only get twenty-five dollars a week," I told Lupe on the way back, "when I can work one time for Snake and make fifty dollars?"

Lupe shrugged. "I know. Shoot, go for it. Just don't forget me. But I still don't like how Snake plays around with people's money or the way he plays around with you. You keep talking about 'my dad, my dad.' *My* dad doesn't treat me like that in public."

I left Lupe back at her house. "Don't forget me about that party tomorrow night," Lupe said. "I bet

Miz Arzalia's gonna tell your aunt everything she saw you do—and said."

"I ain't even studying Miz Arzalia," I said, and was scared all the way home.

I tiptoed into the house, listening hard and looking around. When I reached the back porch, Aretha was stuffing sheets and towels into the drier.

"Is Aunt Limo home yet?"

Aretha shook her head. "But she called again, wanting to know what you were doing. I just said washing clothes. This is the last load." She picked up a basket of dry clothes and took it into the front room.

I followed with another basket. "You said that to her?" I couldn't think of how to tell her thanks for helping me with the clothes. I started to fold clothes and stack them on the couch. "Well, washing clothes is what I've been doing," I said instead, "at least part of the day."

"Yeah, and the rest of it was up at Uncle Snake's. I know because Miz Arzalia and Reverend Reed called to tell Momma where you were. I hope you tell Momma the plain truth when she asks."

"I got nothing to hide." I smoothed a pillowcase. "I need the money."

"Yeah, well, that's true. We all do. Remember how Potsey and me and you and Lupe went all over Deacons Neck last month applying for burger jobs? They said we were too young, but Potsey was old enough. And I've seen Laurice Vereen and them cooking hamburgers. They're no older than we are. These old white stores around here only hire their own relatives' kids. Not us."

"And nobody black in Deacons Neck who has a business'll hire you, either, if you're not kin. Ole country town." I remembered a TV show from Atlanta with kids our age working at all kinds of things. "Wish I lived in a big city. I could do everything and make all kinds of money."

"Keep dreaming." Aretha pointed at the clock. "I hope what Uncle Snake paid you is worth the fussing you're gonna get from Momma when she gets home."

C • H • A • P • T • E • R

6

When Aunt Limo's getting-off-work time neared, I sat down in the front porch swing to watch for her. Aretha followed me.

"How come you think she'll be mad?" I said.

" 'Cause we both know she will, Zambia."

"But technically, I haven't done anything wrong. Number one, Snake's club over here's not a nightclub yet, right? It's not open for business. The sign's not even up. Number two, even if it is a real club, I haven't been inside, so I haven't broken any laws."

"But—"

"Number three, and most important, Aunt Limo's been talking all along about clubs in Gumbo Grove—not over here. So I'm in the clear all the way around." I folded my arms. "Case closed."

"Case is not closed. Number one, two, and three, you're in trouble, and if you try to run that mess past Momma and Daddy, you're gonna be in worse trouble. They know better, and they know that you do too. And *that's* what's gonna make 'em mad."

I uncrossed my arms. "Well, how about number

four: I made some money by honest work. They're always talking about doing things honest."

"No, Zambia. You're wrong all the way around. Can't you see that? Momma told you plain and simple to stay away from Uncle Snake's club and you didn't. Period. Doesn't matter if it's in Gumbo Grove, Deacons Neck, or the North Pole. No *ifs, ands,* or butts, but yours. Good luck." Aretha went back into the house.

I couldn't see it that way, but I guess it didn't matter, because the only way things were going to be looked at was Aunt Limo's and Uncle Lamar's. I pulled the ball of dollar bills from my pocket, ironed them out on my thigh, and counted them. Minus that fifteen dollars to Lupe and what I spent on food, I still had almost thirty-two dollars left—made in just one day.

Just then I saw a big bag and Aunt Limo's pink uniform pants turn the corner up the street. My mouth dried up. Okay, first I'd tell her about hard work, then show her the money, then get Aretha to back me up on how well I did the washing—if she would. I nodded to myself. See what happens from there.

I rolled that over in my head a couple of times. Aunt Limo disappeared into Rev. Reed's grocery store. After about fifteen minutes she came out. Still lugging that big sack, she zigzagged across the street to Miz Arzalia's, then headed on toward me. The sack looked bigger than she did.

"I've been thinking about you, ZamBee," she said when she reached our hedges.

Still holding my money, I ran down to her. "Hey, let me take—ouphf!" I tripped on a clump of grass growing in a crack of the sidewalk and smashed right into her. My nickels, dimes, and dollars went everywhere.

"I washed the clothes," I said, hopping around picking coins out of the grass. "I didn't do *nothing* wrong, because I worked hard at Snake's and here's the money, see? And excuse me for bumping you."

Aunt Limo set the sack on the swing and plumped herself down beside it. She slipped off her tennis shoes and massaged her left foot. "You got anything else to tell me? Or do you want to start at the beginning and explain the whole thing?"

I stepped back into the screen doorway, holding the door ajar. "Probably wouldn't make any difference now what I said. Everybody's already told you a lot of stuff."

"Close the door, Zambia, you're letting in the flies," Aunt Limo said. "Now come sit down in this chair, and quit mumbling." When I did, she stretched out on the swing, then hung one leg over the back of it. "So I'm asking you. From the jump, what have you done today?"

I told her the truth, even the part where Snake hit the man with the rake. "And now you guys are gonna ground me, huh?"

"Do you think that's what you deserve to get?" She stared at me real hard. "No? Oh. The way you talked, I thought you'd done something you knew I wouldn't like." She sat up. "Zambia, you could have called me and got permission to work for your father. It's not like you work for him all the time. You know that. Now listen, for the last time. A club—open, closed, or upside down—is not the place for a twelve-year-old girl to be around. At least, not *you*. Period. I don't care if it's your father's or anybody else's. Snake's not going to keep watch over you on his property any more than he's kept watch over you in any of the other years you've been on this earth. You just now told me he almost hit you with the rake, fussing with somebody."

"That was a mistake. And nothing happened to me. All I did was rake his old yard, and Lupe was with me. He gave me fifty dollars."

"Brother Moneybags." Aunt Limo grunted. "Zam-Bee, I love you like you were my own child. I've asked Snake time and again for help since we got you, but he always had some excuse about not being able to do anything, not even to buy you shoes."

"Oh." I crossed my arms. "But maybe he couldn't, 'cause maybe he had a lot of debts and—"

"No, Zambia. Your father's never had so many debts that he couldn't help take care of you or your mother. He . . . I'm tired of talking about that man."

"Well, if he doesn't have any debts maybe I can go live with him some day, huh?"

Aunt Limo leaned toward me like she hadn't heard. "What? Do what?"

"I mean, maybe sometime. I don't mean like live with him right now, today. But . . . I . . . I was just . . . thinking about it."

Aunt Limo stood up. "After what I just told you, now you want to live with him." She slid on her tennis shoes, leaving her heels out. She picked up the sack. "If you want to go live with your father, Lamar and I won't stand in your way," she said softly. "But you might find living with him to be a whole lot different from what you *think* it is, Sister Hardhead. I'm warning you, honey, a hard head makes a soft behind."

She left me in the chair. What did she mean? I peeked in through the screen door to the front room. Aunt Limo sat on the couch with her eyes closed. She opened them suddenly, looking straight at me, then her face wrinkled up and she began to cry.

I backed up and ended on the porch swing again. I couldn't think of anything to say to make her tears go away. It wasn't supposed to go like this! Aunt Limo wasn't supposed to cry.

Just then a white Jeep sped by with a bunch of boys inside, waving cans of beer. A can flew into our front yard.

"Hey, come pick up your trash!" I yelled. When I went out to get the can, I saw the Jeep do a doughnut in the street, spinning completely around, burning tires. Then it skidded into Snake's parking lot. The boys trooped into the building, leaving the Jeep running and the music still on. It was so loud that I could understand every word in the song. It was boss too.

Lupe's dad came out on his porch. Rev. Reed came to the doorway of her store with her hands on her hips. Mr. Shinshiner leaned forward in his wheelchair.

I cut a few steps to the music in the grass, but stopped when I looked up and saw Aunt Limo at our door too. She shook her head, then went back inside.

Miz Arzalia marched across the street. She knocked on Snake's door. One of the guys walked out with her to the Jeep and cut off the music. Rev. Reed went back into her store, Mr. Gore went back inside his house, and Miz Arzalia marched back home.

I sat down on the porch steps. Everything was dead again. After about five minutes Snake strolled out to the Jeep and turned the music back on full blast.

"Whoa!" I giggled, then sneaked a look around. Guess Miz Arzalia lost on *that* round. But a few minutes later a blue-and-white Deacons Neck police car rolled up the street. The Jeep was blaring away. The police car slowed, turned into the nightclub's front yard, and two cops went into the club. Everybody came back out to their porches and doors and gawked.

In a little bit the cops and my dad left the club, laughing and shaking hands. The officers drove off—but the music continued to play. I waved at Snake, but he must not have seen me. Not even the police could boss my daddy around. My father had pull. Maybe he'd teach me how to have pull too. I snapped my fingers to the beat from the Jeep. This summer was going to be dynamite, and I was going to learn a lot. I wouldn't have to only learn from TV, either. I planned to learn firsthand. Everybody'd have to call me Sister Too-Tough for sure.

That is, if I lived through dinner. I still had to deal with Uncle Lamar and what he'd say about me at Snake's and wanting to move. I felt my forehead. No fever. I couldn't pass up dinner by saying I was sick and avoid him that way. I wasn't on my period, so I couldn't say I had cramps and stay in bed. Plus Aunt Limo was frying pork chops, and I sure didn't want to miss *them*.

I tried to think up things to say to Uncle Lamar—just in case he did come to eat before going on to his second job. What if I said something stupid to him, like I had to Aunt Limo? Then he'd say, "Sis, what's this?" I didn't want to make him feel bad too. Though I knew he wouldn't cry, I sure didn't want to get him upset with me.

Aretha called "Come eat" just then. I flew into the dining room and slid into my chair at the table. Aunt Limo said grace. I kept my eyes on my plate. Dinner went fast, with nobody saying anything. Aretha kept looking at me and then at Aunt Limo. At the end we all jumped up. Aretha and Aunt Limo left the kitchen.

I washed the dinner dishes in record time. In our bedroom Aretha hogged the TV and the fan too. That was another problem in this house—no air-conditioning. I bet Seritta and Meritta were cooling it right now with central air. I lay on my bed, sweating, and tried to think of something to say to Aretha.

"Thanks for helping me with the wash," I finally said. Aretha nodded. She turned the fan a little more my way.

Just about dark we heard a roar outside the house that made us jump off our beds and run to the windows. We didn't see anything, but we heard tires screech in the distance. "I hope nobody got run over," Aretha said, back at her bed.

"Shoot, nobody gets run over in Deacons Neck," I reminded her. "I'd give anything to see a shooting. I mean, not to anybody I know, of course."

Aretha paused from picking at the nail polish on her big toe. "Why? Are you like that girl our age I saw on TV who was so sure she was gonna die from a shooting that she already had her funeral planned? That sounds so violent. And sad."

"No, I just want to see if it's like how people get shot on TV. You know, does a guy's head really explode when he gets shot, and does blood really gush out of his neck, and—"

"You better go to one of those big cities that you're dying to get to. You can see all the violence you want there." Aretha made a face. "You are sick."

I made a face back at her and watched some more TV. I didn't really want to see anybody die. I just wanted to see if "real" was like what we saw on TV. Later on I woke up to Uncle Lamar's car in the driveway. The screen door slammed. He and Aunt Limo began talking in the kitchen. When our bedroom door opened I froze. "The child's asleep," Aunt Limo whispered. "Leave it until tomorrow, Lamar." The door closed.

Close call. Now if I could figure out how to get away from the house tomorrow night and slip over to my dad's grand opening party.

Wednesday morning I waited until Aunt Limo and Uncle Lamar had left for work, then telephoned Lupe. "How can I get to the you-know-what tonight?" I asked her. "And what should I wear?"

"Since you've got no kind of taste in clothes, I don't know." Lupe yawned loud in my ear. "What'd your folks say about you working for your father?"

"Nothing."

"You lie. So, what'd they say about you going to his party?"

"They didn't say I couldn't go."

"You lie again."

"Okay, okay, so they didn't say I could go, but they didn't say I couldn't either."

"Then you're going by yourself. I'm not crazy. Daddy warned me to stay away, and I listen to what *Papacita* says," Lupe said. "And I bet your folks said the same thing."

"But you promised."

"That was before Daddy said no. Sooo . . . let me think. . . . Maybe you and Aretha could get permission to spend the night with me," she finally said. "We could at least stand in the yard."

"That's not going to the party." I let my being mad slide into my voice.

"Best that I can do, *muchacha.*"

"Plus, how'd Aretha get into this? Why's she got to be there?"

"Why not? Your folks aren't dumb. They won't let you be at my house with your dad's big nightclub party going on in your face without Aretha. *You* might not have good sense, but Aretha does. You'll get so excited you could jump out in the street and tear all your clothes off."

"Now, why would I do all that? Okay, okay. So you call Aunt Limo and ask can we stay all night."

"I will not," said Lupe. "Bye."

Next I woke Aretha. "Let's sleep over at Lupe's tonight. She invited us. Would you ask Aunt Limo?"

Aretha yawned and flopped around in her bed. I had to poke her a couple of times to make her understand. She finally mumbled "Okay," then rolled back over on her stomach. Suddenly she sat up. "You haven't fooled *nobody,* ZamBee. You just want to watch the grand opening."

"Well, don't you?" I looked her in the eye hard.

"Shoot, yes." She grinned. "But I'm just letting you know that people's not as dumb around here as you think we are."

Aretha called Aunt Limo and asked. Aunt Limo in effect said yes, but she must have had a lot of "don't do this" and "don't do that," because Aretha said, "Yes, ma'am" and "No, we won't" a million times.

Anyway, so far so good. By four-fifteen I was on my way to Lupe's before Aunt Limo could get home and see that what I wore was not my usual sleep-over clothes. I could see a pink neon sign with black-and-gold lettering that flashed SNAKE'S PARADISE NUMBER TWO hanging from a pole in front of the building all the way from our house. Then I slowed down. Whoa! A black glossy cobra figurine with gold glittery eyes swayed around and around and around on top of the sign. It looked like the kind of sign you'd see in Gumbo Grove at the big-time oceanfront hotel lounges. That huge snake, though, made me shiver.

A few cars, a cable TV truck, and a telephone company van were already parked around the club. As I got to Lupe's, a long beer truck pulled up, the driver hopped out and began stacking cases of beer onto his hand cart.

I tried to peek in through the club's open door, but since I was across the street, I was too far away to see anything. "Oh, my, who're you trying to impress with those clothes?" Lupe said when I walked up to the porch. "If they were on you any tighter they'd be wrapped around your bones."

"You know I'm looking good." I touched my Paradise Number Two visor, then wiggled my behind, which I'd squeezed into pink tights. I was proud of my matching halter top, too, even though I had to keep my tummy sucked in so it wouldn't bulge over the top of my tights. Lupe wore a halter top, too. New!

"The cops have already been over there," Lupe said. "I think they walked all through the place. Then they shook hands with Snake and left."

"Maybe they're his security guards. Or else they're too scared to do anything. When my old man says 'jump,' the cops just ask, 'how high?' "

"Oh, that's so old your great-grandmomma wouldn't even say that," Lupe groaned. "Anyway, Momma and Daddy're bowling tonight. They'll probably go to the VFW afterward. They don't get home till one or two o'clock in the morning. I'm fixing tacos and baloney sandwiches and stuff like that. Wanna help? I know Potsey won't eat. He'll hang right out in the street all night."

I cut cheese triangles and laid them on slices of white bread for myself. Lupe and Aretha were whole wheat nuts. I didn't like that kind because those little spots and seeds looked like the bread had ants all through it.

"Oh, and ZamBee." Lupe paused from stirring the Kool-Aid. "Momma said folks coming to Snake's party are liable to act crazy just to outdo the ones who go to his place in Gumbo Grove. So . . . she said we all gotta stay on the porch."

"What? No way!"

"Look, *Señorita* Too-Tough, I'm staying on the porch, and Momma said anybody who comes to spend the night with me has to stay on the porch, or go back home."

"Is the sidewalk part of the porch?" I asked. "What about the curb?"

Lupe lifted the mustard jar and lined it up with my head. "Zambia, you know what the word *porch* means."

Aretha arrived. She'd changed her clothes too. "Another fashion plate." Lupe eyed Aretha's shorts. "But I still look the best."

Night hit. A steady line of cars pulled up to the club. "Get ready," I said, snapping my fingers. "It's party time tonight!" Snake's security guards guided cars into parking places in the yard that I'd raked. The music inside the club came on, but it stayed low. We waited for action, eating and watching on the porch. But guess what? Nothing happened! Not even a fight! I had to hide my yawns.

"Well, this is a real thrill," Lupe said. "We could have been watching *Roseanne* reruns."

Lupe's folks came home early. "I see the house is still here," Miz Gore said. "Everything go all right over there?"

"It was boring," Lupe said. "Nobody's done anything but go in and go out."

"Good," said Miz Gore. "Hope it stays that way."

Lupe turned to me. "I didn't see Seritta or Meritta outside. Think they were inside?"

"Oh, no," said her mother. "You can't have underage kids inside a club that sells alcohol, not even at a grand opening. It's against the law. They can take the kid, the bar owner, and maybe even the parents to jail. Everybody knows that."

Aretha tapped me on the knee. "Did Seritta know that when she invited you?" she whispered.

"No big deal, Aretha, no big deal." I remembered Snake, the police, and the music this afternoon. I bet Seritta had been inside the club then, but the police hadn't made her leave. Maybe Snake stopped them.

I just wish that I could have been at the party tonight. Then I could have really seen Snake in action. Maybe he even would have introduced me to everybody.

"This is my other girl, Zambia," I imagined him saying. "And real soon she's gonna come live with me, and I'm gonna buy her new clothes and teach her stuff, straight up, and everything'll be def. Everybody, see Zambia? This is my daughter too."

Then everybody would have applauded and looked

jealous. Yeah, I could deal with that. It'd be nice to have somebody I could call Daddy around all the time. Calling somebody Uncle wasn't enough, even if it was Uncle Lamar.

C·H·A·P·T·E·R

7

Vrrrooom! I sat up quick. Sounded like a vacuum cleaner was right under Lupe's window—at seven o'clock on a Thursday morning? Blinking and frowning, Lupe sat up too. When I looked out the window, I saw a man with a huge leaf-blowing machine across the street at the club, blowing paper and other junk from Snake's party last night out of the club's yard. He didn't pick up the mess, though, so it rolled this way to Lupe's side of the street.

"Hey!" Lupe hollered out the window. "Turn that thing off, waking people up!" The man didn't pay her any attention. Aretha, who died when she went to sleep, didn't even wake up. Lupe and I grabbed up our pillows and plopped on the couch in the rec room in the back of the house.

After a while I fell off to sleep, and woke up with Lupe's feet in my face. The house was quiet. Lupe's folks had left. So had Snake's stupid no-cleaning-up-cleanup man. I crept off the couch into Lupe's room, changed clothes, and headed outside. Snake's Jeep sat across the street. I strolled over to the curb. Beer cans, chicken bones, bread crusts, and gum wrappers lined the curb.

Just then Seritta came out of the club. A thick red braid hung down each side of her face. Lucky! As I raised my hand to wave she turned around and went back in. Was that a snub or what? I sneaked a look around at Lupe's house and saw the front room curtains twitch. I made myself hang around in the yard. After what seemed like forever, Seritta came back out.

"What's happening?" I said real loud, to make sure she heard and saw me. "Boss party, huh? Didn't see you last night."

Seritta slid into the Jeep. "Hey, I didn't see you either. We were humping, girl, all night long, helping Daddy until three o'clock this morning," she said.

"I saw you just now, but I guess you didn't see me." I wished I could have helped Snake last night too.

"Is this a quiz or something?" Seritta snapped, then grinned. "Sorry. I didn't see you just now. I was looking for the car keys. I thought I'd lost them and I sure didn't want Daddy to be mad."

"They told me kids couldn't come inside the club." I was going to check this out once and for all. "Against the law. So how come you can get inside?"

"You believe everything people tell you?" she asked, still smiling.

"No," I said slowly. "Not everything. Some things."

"Yeah, well, what I do doesn't fit under that 'law,' " she said. "And you can believe that." She honked the Jeep horn. "Come on, Daddy. Look, we'll be open every night except Sundays from now on. We're gonna be the bossest place in the whole county. Come on over, sis."

"You must have heard Uncle Lamar call me sis," I said. Hearing her say it made me smile a little.

"Yeah, I did. It's kind of cute," she said.

"You think Snake might give me a job too?" I asked.

Seritta stopped smiling. Then she nodded, like she really was thinking it over. "Maybe. You never know where you can get a gig these days."

Yeah, I told myself, Snake and Daughters, Inc. I liked the sound of that too.

Potsey rode up to us on his bike, with his radio blasting reggae. His brown ponytail bounced in time to the music. He made a little motion with his forefinger and thumb at Seritta. She made it back at him. He winked at her. She winked back.

"What's happenin', Eduardo?" I broke into that game quick!

"Hey, Foxy," he said.

Just then Snake bounced out of the club. The white panama hat, white shirt, white baggy pants, and white shoes he wore made him look like he'd just got off the boat from the Bahamas or somewhere. His gold snake necklace glittered. My daddy was fine! He got into the Jeep next to Seritta.

"ZamBee, my girl, the yard looked good yesterday," he told me. "You do me right, I'll do you right, straight up, square, anything, anytime."

They screeched away.

Bingo! There it was. He said he'd do me right anytime! All I needed to do, then, was ask—for anything!

Potsey was there to hear it. I kicked my foot a couple of times to the music, then threw in an extra couple of steps for Potsey's benefit. Snake and Daughters, Inc. would be out of sight! Look at Sister Too-Tough Brown now!

"You trying out for Snake's buck-naked shows?" Smiling, Potsey folded his arms across his chest and slid his hands under his armpits. "Look here, little mama, when're you gonna get enough shape so I can really have something to look at?"

"Look now." I twirled and kicked a couple more times.

"If you'd been at Snake's dancing like that last night I might have looked then," he said. "Where were you? All the other little foxes were in there."

"Your momma told me personally that kids're too young to go in there and she didn't want to go to jail."

"She said that for you and Lupe's benefit, not mine. Snake's Paradise Number Two is gonna be the hottest wave in town. It's got a little room in the back with a dance floor just for under twenty-ones. No alcohol or nothing. That's where me and everybody was. Except for you babies on the porch." He laughed, then slapped one big brown hand over his mouth.

Jealous, I stopped dancing. "So? We had things to do over on your front porch."

"Well, later, ZamBee." Potsey pulled off on his bike. "Stay sweet."

Talk about my heart flipping and flopping! "Boy, I'll stay sweet for you forever!" I told him. "Just come be mine,'' I added to myself, and danced back to Lupe's house.

"What's a *who*?'' Lupe asked at breakfast. "I never heard of a buck-naked club. What else did Potsey talk about? What room? What? Get outta here!'' She poked out her lips. "See, Potsey gets to do everything. I don't get to do *nothing*.'' She kicked her thong across the room.

"You know why,'' Aretha said. " 'Cause he's a boy.''

"I can barely get in and out of the yard without Daddy running a virginity check on me,'' Lupe said. "What could happen to me in ole dead Deacons Neck? We haven't had a shooting in five years, and they say that one was an accident. I'm gonna start doing whatever I want too.'' She snapped her fingers at Aretha. "Think of something bad we can do,'' she said.

"We?'' Aretha said. "*You*. Go bungee jumping. Your folks sure don't want you to do that.''

"I don't either. Next?''

"You could get pregnant, like Tonya and Barbara Ann did,'' said Aretha.

"No, no, no!'' Clutching her stomach, Lupe fell back in her chair.

"Hitchhike to Charleston,'' I said. "No, to Atlanta. No, New York. Go to Hollywood and be a rapper.''

"That's *your* thing, ZamBee,'' Lupe said. "Next?''

"Okay, okay.'' Aretha waved her hands in the air. "Get dressed up like you're new in town—''

"And go into the Paradise on the next Thursday when Ladies Night gets started,'' I broke in.

"No. I was gonna say spend the day in the video arcade at the mall," Aretha said.

"Aretha, I do that anyway." Lupe chewed slowly. "I'm thinking on what you said, ZamBee. Naw. I don't wanna go in the club *that* bad. Not yet. I don't like that snake spinning around up there either. There's something funny about that place."

"Now, what's the building done to you?" I asked.

"I don't like seeing that big cobra through my window all night," Lupe said. "I was used to that old red rooster weather vane on top of the garage."

Aretha blew cereal across the table, laughing. Then I had to laugh at her. We helped Lupe clean up the kitchen and her bedroom, then left.

I wished I had a real job—not like Uncle Lamar's or Aunt Limo's, though. Aunt Limo and Uncle Lamar worked all the time. It seemed like they hardly ever had any money to do anything with. Mornings, Aunt Limo cleaned rooms at the Twilight Motel. Afternoons she'd clean at the Sweet Night Inn. On some weekends she helped to cater at private parties. In the wintertime she helped at the nursing home. Once in a while in the winter she'd get a call to be a substitute teacher in the schools. To teach was what she really wanted to do, but the school system wouldn't hire her. She had her certificate and everything. Jobs were hard to get in the winter.

"I hadn't thought about how slow it was on this street until the nightclub opened up," Aretha said as we walked home. "Now a lot more cars go through. Wish I had a car. I'd go everywhere." Just then a little blue car rolled past us, music pounding. "Like that one," she said. "Did you see the driver? He was fine, girl."

"That old man? He must have been twenty years old."

"Well, maybe he has a younger brother. I could learn to like older men."

She was quiet, then, "ZamBee, I been wanting to ask you. Do you still want to live with Uncle Snake?"

I nodded, wondering where this conversation was headed.

"Well, how come? 'Cause he's got money? Or just 'cause you don't like it here with us no more?"

"No, it's like . . . well, he *is* my dad, Aretha. I—I don't know how to put it into words." How could I tell her I wanted someone that I could call Daddy and be around too? She had Uncle Lamar to call Dad, even if he did wear old fogey clothes and work all the time. At least she had him at home with her every night, and she could hear him snoring. From watching Lupe and Mr. Gore, and Aretha and Uncle Lamar, it was kind of cool having a dad. I liked how Uncle Lamar teased Aretha sometimes, which he never did with me. And Lupe would just go up to her dad and hug him, and ask him how she looked in clothes. I never felt like I could ask Uncle Lamar about how I looked, ever. I wondered what he'd say if I did?

"I was just gonna say that you can watch my TV more if you want, and I won't say a word." She added, "I mean, if you want to stay."

"Really? Uncle Lamar said that that TV's for both of us anyway," I said. "But, I mean, thanks."

We reached the house and started on our own chores. It was almost noon on another dull Thursday in Deacons Neck.

A week staggered by. More cars drove by, playing their music loud, on their way to my dad's club. I was washing, scrubbing, and watching for my father to get another chance to talk to him. Meanwhile, things stayed like a morgue.

Come the next week, on Wednesday morning, Aretha was moaning over all the clothes she had to wash. "And we're out of bleach. ZamBee, would you go get some?"

I held out my hand. "Momma didn't leave me any money," she said. "Maybe Reverend Reed will let you have it on credit."

"Okay," I said, glad to get out of the house. "Be right back." On the way I saw Snake standing in the nightclub yard. I noticed that his trash barrel was on its side, and junk was everywhere. By now he'd been open two weeks. I walked right over to the curb on his side. "Hey . . . uh . . . Dad, if I pick up the trash and cans, will you pay me? 'Course, Aunt Limo doesn't want me to work for you."

He shrugged. "That's between you and Miss Limousine. If you can handle where you want to go, go where you want. You wanna do my trash, then fine, hop to it."

I cleared my throat. "But I gotta get paid, and like you said get it straight up front how much."

"I'll pay you ten dollars. You ought to get it squared with Limo somehow," he said. "Though I figure you ought to be old enough to know what you want to do."

My face got hot and sweaty. Was this one of his trick questions or a compliment? "Well, I . . . I . . ." I wet my lips. "You think maybe I could, uh, come by your house, or uh, stay with you all sometime?"

He waved at a man in a red minivan that had started to back up toward us. "I say 'stay where you want when you want' is how I feel, anytime," he told me. "Hey, Raoul, my man!" When the van reached him, Snake took a small plastic bag out of his pocket and handed it through the window. The van roared away.

"I can? So are you saying that I can come live with you guys?" My stomach started shaking. Snake turned back toward me with his mouth open to speak. But when an old white beat-up car pulled up, he hopped over to the car, got in, and the car sped away. I hurried over to Rev. Reed's store, got the bleach on credit, shot it up to Aretha, and hurried back to the club. I knew what Snake had told me—but was he telling the truth? Sure sounded like it to me!

Boy, that thought made me break out in goose bumps. Me and my dad! So maybe he hadn't forgotten me. Maybe he had saved a little something for me after all.

I set the city garbage barrel upright, then started dropping cans, bottles, and cups back into it. I tried to be speedy, like how he wanted.

After I finished, at first I waited at the side of the nightclub, hoping nobody would see me in his yard and tell Uncle Lamar. Then I crossed the street and sat on Lupe's porch, waiting.

Snake did come back, but before I could even get off the porch he left again in a waiting telephone company truck. I patted my foot and tried not to get irritated. Miz Gore came to the door. "Hi, Zambia. Lupe's at the mall. She'll be back later."

"Oh, okay," I said.

Snake returned just then. I stood up, glanced at Miz Gore, then sat back down. Miz Gore looked at me, then over at Snake. She stayed by her door, so I stayed where I was, too. Finally Snake drove away, this time in his Jeep. Miz Gore went back inside. Darn!

After about an hour my father returned. I flashed down the steps. Snake aimed the Jeep over toward me on Lupe's side of the street. "Thanks," he said. Squeezing my hand, he handed me the ten dollars.

"Thanks. This is like, uh, Snake and Daughters, Inc.," I said. He smiled at me a little and revved the engine. "Do you like my blouse?" I asked him.

"What? Sure. Later, girl." He drove off.

As I watched him drive away, my heart almost exploded with pride. That squeeze was almost as good as a hug. I wished I could tell Aunt Limo. It was more than what Uncle Lamar had done lately.

Aunt Limo. I blew out my breath. I'd just done what she said not to do again—to stay away from the club. Now what was I gonna say?

I went over to Rev. Reed's grocery store for a pop. Now I could even pay her for the bleach. I picked up two of her signs that had slipped from the screen door.

One said THIS BUSINESS IS A NEIGHBORHOOD CRIME-WATCH SITE. The other said BLUE STAR, which meant that the place was supposed to be safe for kids to come to if they were in trouble and couldn't get home.

Rev. Reed stopped stacking cigarettes on the shelf to take the signs. "Are you staying smart and pretty for me? Have a Coke and some potato chips on me."

I watched her snuggle the packs up against each other. "Thanks. Reverend Reed, I've been wanting to ask you something. You say people shouldn't smoke. So how come you sell cigarettes?"

"Well, I certainly don't sell them to minors, and I *can* sell them legally. Is that what you mean?"

"No. You said a person's body is a temple and we should keep our temples clean. Aren't you helping folks dirty up their temples?"

"Oh. I . . . well . . . hmmm." She coughed a couple of times, cleared her throat, and scratched her head. "I keep cigarettes and chewing tobacco for the convenience of our senior citizens who don't want to leave the neighborhood."

"Yeah, but if they get cancer, won't you feel bad?"

"But, Zambia, I . . . oh, dear." She sighed. "You're absolutely right. I can't have one set of principles for the pulpit and a different set for every day, can I?"

I shook my head, pleased that I was right for once and she was wrong.

"On the other hand, a lot of my business depends on tobacco. If I stop selling cigarettes I might have to go out of business. And they'll just buy the cigarettes someplace else."

"So sell something that folks'll buy enough of."

"Like what? Beer and wine? No, no." She leaned against the refrigerator. "What do you suggest?"

I pretended to read the label on a can of pork and beans. "I don't know. I was just asking."

"Thanks for pointing out my problem. I wish you'd point out a solution. But I'll think about it. I don't want to live my life in a way that makes me look like a hypocrite."

I could see that she was getting warmed up for a sermon. I didn't have time for that. I didn't want her to go out of business either.

"You try to fight the battles that you think you might win, see," Rev. Reed said. "I try to save souls. I try to fight pollution. So think, Zambia, think. Right now you're polluting your body with my pop and potato chips. If I stocked broccoli and carrots instead, which are good for you, would you buy them?"

I stopped chewing. "Heck, no." I set the can of pop down. "Reverend Reed, would you ask Aunt Limo something for me?"

"It depends," she said. "What?"

"Ask her if I can work for Snake. He said I could, but she doesn't want me to be around him."

Rev. Reed walked behind the counter, sat down, and propped her elbows on the top. She rested her face on her hands. "Come sit and let's talk for real. What would you be doing for Snake, and when, and where?"

I slid onto the stool across from her. "Raking, picking up cans and bottles in his yard, junk like that." Outside, through the screen door, I saw two men on the sidewalk looking toward the store. I didn't know who they were. When a police car passed by, they walked away. I turned back to Rev. Reed. "I helped him before. You saw me, remember? He gave me fifty dollars and said I did a good job. Maybe we can go into business and be Snake and Daughters, Inc., or something. I did some work for him just now. He paid me ten dollars."

"Mr. Moneybags. Let me think about this." She drummed her fingers on the counter, then pulled on one of the dreadlocks hanging out from under her scarf. "Zambia, I wish the Lord could make it so that I could hire you, but I can't even pay myself a salary half the time. It's not Snake himself so much, but what he represents that bothers your folks. That club is trouble. Lots of parents who found out that their kids were at Snake's party don't want that kind of influence on their children."

"Yeah, but Lupe's folks were at the VFW. Shouldn't they have stayed home, away from all that booze? People get in trouble at the VFW too."

"True. It's just as bad. I'm on your side. Look, Limo and Lamar aren't trying to keep you from your dad. It's . . . well, he just doesn't have a history of doing much good for anybody." She stopped. "That didn't sound right. Your folks should be talking to you about your father, not me."

"He's got a big house, two nightclubs, three or four cars. Sounds like he's helping Seritta and them a lot."

Rev. Reed rested her hand on my shoulder. "But you don't know what really goes on inside that big house and those clubs."

I frowned. "Do you?"

"Yes."

"What?"

Rev. Reed tilted her head to the side and pooched out her lips. "I know Snake beats on Sissy. That he's beat on Seritta and Meritta. I know this for a fact."

"Seritta never said anything about it to me."

"Why should she? It's nothing to be proud of."

"Well, maybe she did something wrong. Maybe she—"

"Zambia, it's abuse, and it's wrong. Period. As your pastor, I want to lead you the right way. As your friend, I want to help you. Can I tell you about my very best friend? It'll just take a minute. Okay?"

I nodded, sighing. I couldn't believe that Snake would hit his wife and his kids. "I don't see how this is going to help me get a job and go stay with my father, though."

"Stay with your father?" Rev. Reed blinked. "Oh, now I see what this is all about. Listen. This girl was my very best friend. Pretty, smart, just like you. We started running with a crowd. The boy she thought could rock her world got her and some other kids strung out on heroin and cocaine. Right here in little bitty countrified Deacons Neck. Somehow, praise God, I didn't.

"My friend got hooked so bad that she turned against her family, friends, even me. She'd get so stoned sometimes, she couldn't even take a bath or comb her hair. When she got pregnant and had his baby, he took up with another girl. My girlfriend started stealing to buy drugs. That boy had money, but he wouldn't give her a dime, not even to help with the baby. He even bragged that the baby wasn't his, even though it looked just like him."

I listened close. "That girl was stupid. She should have just taken his money."

"How?"

I shrugged. "I don't know. Like how they do on those soap operas. So anyway, what happened after that?"

"She got arrested. He's still running around. She's in bad shape even today. I pray for her all the time. I pray for him too, but I never thought much of that creep, and he knows it."

"Is that the end of the story? I thought you were gonna say she got shot or stabbed, or that she killed him or something. What happened to the baby?"

"What do you think happened?" Rev. Reed said.

I shrugged. "I guess it just grew up or something." Then suddenly I knew what she was getting at. "I don't run with *no* druggies, just Aretha, Lupe, Potsey, and Seritta. I'm not like that girl. No way!"

"Oh, but you are," she said. "That's why you're so precious to me. I just pray that you'll know enough not to take the same road that she did. Think, ZamBee, think."

C · H · A · P · T · E · R

8

As I returned from Rev. Reed's a strange man in the back of a music-thumping, white tracker Jeep pointed his forefinger and thumb at me—like Potsey had with Seritta. I didn't know what that signal meant, but when I did it back, the car slowed and backed up. I giggled and got nervous.

He touched the bill of his Atlanta Braves baseball cap. "Well?"

"Well what?" Still walking, I stuck my hands in my pockets.

"You sweet little ole tenderoni, come on over here. I can give you a good time. Won't cost you a thing this time."

"Naw." I strolled on slow like I didn't have a care in the world. The car rolled beside me for a few yards with the man still talking, then drove on. My heart thumped along with the music. I was glad I had my tightest blue jeans on. He said I was fine! I couldn't wait to tell Lupe and Aretha.

The Jeep turned around in the middle of the street, passed me again, then continued on to Snake's. Two men standing in front of the nightclub waved at me. "Hey, sugar, what's your name?" one yelled.

"None ya." I kept on walking, but I couldn't help grinning. Silver Dollar Road was popping today! And my daddy's club was making it pop.

About that time I saw Uncle Lamar's car in the driveway. Oh-oh, things were gonna pop at home too. What was he doing home this time of the day, and on a Wednesday? He hardly ever came home for lunch. I burned on down that street for the house, trying to think of how to explain why I hadn't cleaned up the kitchen yet. But when I edged into the living room, I saw Aunt Limo. She lay on the couch, eyes closed, covered by a sheet. Uncle Lamar and Aretha sat by her on kitchen chairs. "Hey, what's the matter? What's happened?" I asked.

Uncle Lamar pressed his finger to his lips. "She broke her ankle, sis. We just got her back from the hospital. And where have you been?"

"Up at Reverend Reed's store." My heart pounding, I squatted down by the couch to be close to Aunt Limo. "Is she gonna be all right? Is she hurting bad?"

"Anytime you break bones it's gonna give you pain," he said. "They wanted to keep her in the hospital overnight, but since we don't carry health insurance, they wanted me to give them a bunch of money up front. I couldn't do that. When she wakes up we'll move her to the bed."

Uncle Lamar slumped back in his chair. "What next?" he said. The telephone rang. When Aretha stood up he told her, "No, I'll get it."

He went to the telephone in the kitchen. He stood in the doorway talking on the telephone, watching Aunt Limo all the time.

"Yeah, I know, but you can't hold that woman back," he said into the telephone. "She was working those jobs to save enough money for a down payment on that house she's been wanting, but I think that's on hold now. Limo wanted so bad to get off Silver Dollar Road, especially now that that club's open."

Aretha and I blinked at each other. "Another house?" Aretha whispered.

"And where is it?" I whispered back.

I sat down where Uncle Lamar had been. "How'd she break her ankle, Retha?"

"She was trying to get across Ninth Street, where that real steep curb is, twisted her ankle, then went down on it. She told us that a truck stopped not six inches from her head."

I shivered. Suddenly Uncle Lamar hollered into the telephone, glaring at me. "Well, Rev. Reed, Miss Zambia might as well forget it. What? Why?"

Aretha groaned. "Now what'd you do?" she whispered.

"Nothing." I kept my eyes on Aunt Limo's face. "So she was walking fast the way she always does, and it was hot, and she probably wasn't looking where she was stepping—"

"And boom! Down she went! Poor Mamma." Aretha wiped Aunt Limo's sweaty forehead with a damp cloth. "I bet she'll lose her jobs again. Remember last summer, when she was working two jobs on the beach and had to catch Mr. Prioleau's van at four o'clock every morning?"

I nodded. "And got dog sick for four days off some ole germ she inhaled from tourists coughing in her face."

"Just when Momma got better and found two more jobs, Daddy's night job stopped," Aretha said. "Seems like we have the worst luck."

Last winter Aunt Limo found out she'd been hired to substitute teach twice a week for a month in the schools. Boy, she was on top of the world. But then she had some kind of female problem and had to have an emergency operation. She lost the teaching job, and most of the money they'd saved up to help get us through the winter went on the hospital bill. Uncle Lamar got laid off for a month from his day job at the peanut factory. The water pipes froze and busted, too, and that made another big bill.

They tried to keep their money problems a secret from Aretha and me, but how? We had eyes and ears. They got so deep in debt that our electricity and our heat were cut off, right in the middle of January.

"I hope we don't have to freeze again." Aretha must have read my mind. "That old heating company was nasty, refusing to deliver oil unless we could pay off the whole heating bill. I found out later that Momma borrowed the money from Uncle Snake."

"Oh, really?" I stared at her. "Who said so?"

"Momma. Daddy didn't want to use the money. Momma paid him back, though."

Uncle Lamar made Aunt Limo go to Social Services

to get food stamps, then he stamped around the house and cussed for two weeks afterward and wouldn't eat the food she bought with the stamps.

"And then remember," said Aretha, "how we had to stand in line for two hours downtown to pick up a box of emergency food in all that freezing cold because they'd only let two people at a time into the building?"

"Yeah, like we were going to steal their ole moldy cheese and concrete-tasting macaroni. I hope we don't have to go through another winter like that again." I glanced at Uncle Lamar talking low on the telephone. "We've got to get some jobs. Reverend Reed said she needed someone to scrub and sweep, but then she said she didn't have any money."

"So what kind of job is that?" Aretha said. When Aunt Limo moaned in her sleep, we moaned along with her and stopped talking.

A whole ten minutes went by. It seemed like an hour. After Uncle Lamar finally got off the telephone, he walked in and looked down at Aunt Limo lying like a little lump under the sheet with that big white cast up to her knee.

"Well, I'm gone again to work. Call me if you need me. And nobody"— he pointed his finger at me—"nobody else leave this house. Zambia, I need to talk to you when I get back tonight."

I wanted to tell him that with Aunt Limo hurt I didn't want to even leave the room. I was kind of glad when he left, though. What kind of talking-to was he going to give me? Because I worked for my father again? Because I wanted to leave? Because I thought he was dull and old-fashioned? He hardly ever talked to me about something I did wrong. He usually left it up to Aunt Limo. I could remember only once when Uncle Lamar ever got after Aretha for something, and boy, when he was through, Aretha's face was puffy and full of tear trails. I sure didn't want to go through that.

Aretha and I tiptoed around the couch the rest of Wednesday afternoon. I even helped Aretha finish up the wash. When I heard music blaring outside, I went to the screen door, frowning. "I wish they'd shut that stuff off," I said. "Don't they know we got sickness in here?" Then I saw that the music came from Snake's minivan as it rolled up the street.

The telephone rang again. Aretha beat me to it. "No, she's asleep," she said. She said "I don't know" three or four times, then hung up. "That was Momma's motel boss. He said if she couldn't come back to work by Monday that she might as well not come back at all. I better call Daddy."

When Aunt Limo woke up, Aretha and I tried to get her to move to her bed, but she wouldn't go. She wouldn't eat either. She just tossed and turned on the couch. "Man, it feels like my leg's being ate up by worms," she whispered. "Retha, ZamBee, somebody, hand me that bottle of pain pills."

She wouldn't even move to her bedroom when Uncle Lamar came home for dinner Wednesday evening. I stayed out of Uncle Lamar's way. He was so busy with Aunt Limo he forgot about our talk.

It was like that all day Thursday, too, with Aunt Limo moaning and in pain, and me and Aretha not knowing what to do, and Uncle Lamar just looking sad and working. It seemed like every car with a big engine or a big sound system cruised up and down our street all evening long. Thursday night featured Ladies Night at Snake's Paradise Number Two. That meant ladies got into the club for free. Talk about a noisy street! I didn't know ladies could be that loud. When I finally went to bed, I could still hear music and loud voices coming from everywhere outside.

Then around two or three o'clock Friday morning, Aretha woke me up. "They're going crazy outside," she said. "Look!"

When I peeked out the window I saw cars parked every which way on both sides of the road, even in front of our house. People walked up and down our street. Some folks even stood in front of our house talking and laughing.

"I bet Snake's having another party," I whispered.

"Yeah, and I bet Momma can't sleep because of it," Aretha said. "I know Daddy isn't. He's stamping all over the house. He even called the police about the loud music, but it's still loud. Daddy's so upset over Momma being sick and Uncle Snake's club that he's about crazy."

Remembering Aunt Limo, I stopped smiling. "How's she doing?"

"Still tossing and turning and hurting," Aretha said. I leaned by the window, watching. I could feel the music vibrating through the walls. Maybe if Snake had known Aunt Limo was sick he wouldn't have had the party. Or maybe he knew and couldn't change the date. Or maybe . . .

After we got up later that morning and came into the living room to check on Aunt Limo, we saw Uncle Lamar trying to get her to sit up.

"How're you feeling?" I asked her. She tried to smile at me, then just shook her head.

"Momma, you need some more medicine?" Aretha asked.

"Something about her leg's not right," Uncle Lamar said. "She's still in too much pain. I'm gonna take her back to the hospital. You all got to help me get her to the car."

Together we lifted her to her feet. She groaned with each move. Uncle Lamar carried her out the door and down the steps. We helped her into the hatchback part of the Datsun. She was sweating and breathing hard.

"Wait, Uncle Lamar." I ran into the house for a washcloth and a comb. Gently I wiped Aunt Limo's face and ran the comb through her hair. "You're gonna be all right, aren't you?"

"Yeah, baby," she whispered. "You mind Uncle Lamar now, and don't be a hardhead, you hear? Aretha, you behave and don't be bossy."

"Yes, Momma," said Aretha. She looked like she was going to cry. She turned around so I couldn't see her face, and pointed at the yard.

"Looks like the garbage truck dumped on us," she said. Chicken bones, fish skeletons, flies, barbecued rib bones, candy-bar wrappers, ants, cigarette butts, watermelon rinds, paper napkins, beer bottles, plastic cups, and pop cans lay in the road and in people's yards, including ours.

Uncle Lamar looked at Snake's blue minivan at the club. He pressed his lips together. "You girls clean up this trash," he said in a low voice. He and Aunt Limo drove off.

As we picked up the mess, cars began driving up and down the street, pulling into the Paradise parking lot. "Is he open already?" Aretha asked. "It's not even eight o'clock."

"Maybe he didn't close," I said. Somebody needed to talk to Snake's customers. They didn't have to be this nasty, especially not from Ladies Night last night. And what happened to that dude with the leaf blower?

Miz Arzalia, Mr. Gore, and Lupe were picking up trash too, while Potsey leaned on his bike, watching. When I hollered at him, he rode over. A big flashy chain hung down on his handsome chest.

"I *do* like that chain," Aretha said. "Can I have it?"

"Don't even try it," Potsey said. He touched a beeper on his belt a couple of times to make sure we saw it, then reached into a little beaded leather bag on his bike and pulled out a pack of cigarettes. "They partied hard last night, ladies."

"And we get to pick up the mess they left behind," Aretha said.

"When'd you get that beeper? When'd you start smoking?" I asked. "Smoking's nasty."

Potsey shrugged. He tapped the beeper, and waved a cigarette around, but didn't light it. "They're gonna party tonight too. Friday night! Everybody's coming to

Snake's now. There's even some dudes from Atlanta and Charleston here. Man, the Snake knows everybody. I hear he goes to New York, Miami, everywhere."

When Aretha bent down, squinting in the dirt, I looked too. "What're you gawking at? Money?" I said.

"Right there, one of those plastic things, like the ones we see over on Garvey in Gumbo Grove," she said. "A crack vial." She nudged it with her foot.

That's exactly what it looked like to me too. "Don't touch it. Slide a piece of paper under it and throw it in the garbage," I said.

"Whoa!" Potsey hopped off his bike, picked up the vial, and wiped the dirt off. "ZamBee, when you asked if Aretha had found money, you were right. This"—he held up the container—"*is* money."

"You better throw that thing away before it gets you in trouble," I said.

"Throw it away? I'm just helping the environment." He got on his bike and carefully put the vial in his leather pouch.

"How're you gonna help the environment with crack?" Aretha asked.

" 'Cause I'm gonna recycle it." Laughing, he poked his forefinger and thumb at us, then rode up the street to the Paradise.

"We better tell Lupe," Aretha said. "She'll tell her folks and they'll take that stuff away from him. This kind of trouble Potsey definitely does not need."

"Potsey just picked it up to impress us," I said. "He probably threw it away as soon as he got down the street."

■

Aunt Limo stayed in the hospital Friday night, which was probably best because, as Potsey predicted, the street heaved with cars and loud music. And guess what?

Saturday morning when we came outside our yard was so trashy that the garbage we'd picked up Friday must have crawled right back to the same spots. There we were, dragging garbage bags behind us again, picking up junk. We also found a hypodermic needle and a bag of crack. This time we threw them in the garbage can. We called the hospital to talk with Aunt Limo, but another woman answered and said she was asleep.

When Uncle Lamar came home around noon on Saturday to check on us, Aretha told him what we'd found. He pounded the table with his fist, then called the police department. That conversation didn't last long. "They said there wasn't much they could do unless I see somebody with the drugs," he said. "Then I'm supposed to get a description of the person, take down the license plate number of the car they get into, and then sign a warrant for their arrest. How'm I gonna do all that in the middle of the night? That's what the cops are being paid to do!"

Then he called Rev. Reed. That conversation didn't last long either. "She said she found the same things in the backyard of her grocery store and in the church parking lot," he told us. "Miz Arzalia did too."

I leaned up against the wall, listening and watching. Snake's customers again. They just didn't have any smarts. Maybe Snake could put up NO LITTERING and NO

DRUGS signs. Maybe he could make folks not bring drugs over to Silver Dollar Road in the first place. I mean, it was making him look bad, like everything was all his fault. I wanted him to look as good to everybody—especially Uncle Lamar—as he did to me. Snake and Daughters, Inc. didn't seem like such a good idea right now.

Uncle Lamar glanced at me. He tucked his shirt down in his pants. "Zambia, sit down."

Uh-oh, I told myself, here it comes. I took my time finding a chair and settling myself. "What?" I said, and rolled my eyes at him.

When he started out with "Snake and his nightclub are causing problems on our street," I crossed my legs and folded my arms across my chest. "Reverend Reed tells me that now you want to work for him. How could you think of doing such a thing?"

His voice was low, but I could tell that he was mad from the way he kept poking out his lower lip when he talked. "His crooks throw this crap all over our neighborhood for you kids to find, and he pays you to pick it up. You and him got Limo so upset she can't think straight. She was probably thinking about Snake and you when she broke her ankle."

"Is this the talking-to?" I asked. I raised my eyebrows and nodded once at him, the way Snake did.

"Well, one thing you and him's got in common is a smart mouth."

"If my dad was so awful, Aunt Limo wouldn't be taking up for him, would she? He's her brother too." I fought off the tears welling up in my eyes.

"Well, he's not much of one, I can tell you that," Uncle Lamar said back. "I don't understand how you can sit there and not see what's going on or pay any attention to what we're trying to tell you. I've been trying to raise you right. Seems like you'd rather argue with me over this guy. He's bad news, Zambia."

"Well, I can't understand why you got to call him names and say bad things like it's all his fault." I jumped up. "You don't understand either. He's rich and got sharp clothes and big cars and gives me money, and . . . and, no matter what, he's still my dad!"

"If he was all that great, he'd have given you his last name too, but he didn't!" Uncle Lamar jumped up. "Look out, ZamBee. You're hollerin' at the wrong man now. Not in my own house. I've fed and clothed you since you were four years old when your own daddy wouldn't." He shook his finger at me. "And no, I don't have the cash that Snake flashes around, but my money's honest and legal. You're so stupid and hard-headed that you can't see nothing but that flash. There's nothing under his flash but evil ways."

"See, you keep talking mean about him. Snake said I could go live with him if I wanted, and he'll buy me all kinds of stuff, and he won't want me to have to stay here *no* more." I stamped out of the living room into the kitchen and started throwing spoons and forks around. I snatched at a chair.

It fell in front of Uncle Lamar, who had followed me. "Have you gone crazy? You're not gonna tear up what little I got over a dog like Snake." He grabbed me and shook me so hard, my lips bounced up and down. "Don't you talk to me like that!"

"I don't have to stay here," I screamed. "I hate you!"

"You hate me?" When he let me go, I slumped back against the sink. "You hate *me*? That guy fed your momma cocaine till she went crazy, then turned her out in the street to be a hooker—he made your aunt cry over him all her life . . . and you hate *me*? Then you go on to him! Go on!"

I stayed hunched up by the dirty dishes, scared he was going to shake me again or worse, tell me other awful stuff about my dad.

Uncle Lamar snatched up his cap and jammed it down on his head. "I've tried to raise you like a father would, but I don't want *nobody* in my house who won't respect me. He's your father, true, but he's no good. You'll never get that through your hard head till he whops you on it."

After he left the room, I wiped my face on a paper towel and blew my nose. Uncle Lamar told me to go, didn't he? God, now I'd have to! I pressed my lips together to keep away the fear. Well, I'd show *him*. I'd go, all right—I'd go right over to my father's club and tell my father I was ready for him to take me in, like he said he would.

I ran out the back door and ran down the street, passing Miz Arzalia and half a dozen cars on the way. When I saw Snake's Jeep in the yard, I was double thankful that he was there this early on Saturday afternoon. This time I ran straight to the nightclub door and banged on it. He'd understand if I talked to him, straight up.

Snake came to the door. His hair was sticking up all over his head. White sleep crust or something was sprinkled around his nose. He squinted at me through bloodshot eyes. "Yeah? What? What you want?" He looked so bombed-out that at first I couldn't say anything. What had he been doing? Sleeping? "I ain't got all day." He frowned and rubbed his hand over his face. "What now, girl?"

"Uncle—Uncle Lamar beat me up and kicked me out and I wanna stay with you," I stammered.

"Uh-uh—I'm kinda busy right now, Zambia. You work it out with Lamar for now, and uh, we'll talk about it later, okay? That's right, straight up." He closed the door in my face.

I stared at the closed door. He had promised! When I banged again I heard a woman's voice from inside who sure didn't sound like Sissy saying something, and then Snake's voice.

"Renelda's stupid kid," I heard him say. He laughed real loud. "Shuh, I ain't got time for that."

I stumbled away from the club in shock. When I noticed that people on the street were staring at me, I rubbed at my wet face, straightened my blouse, and smoothed down my hair for the long walk back to Uncle Lamar's house. The sidewalk was hot on my bare feet. I walked along in a daze. How could Snake have done that to me? He'd promised! But he called me stupid, like he didn't care about what happened to me. And laughed at me!

When I saw Uncle Lamar's car still in the driveway, I slipped into the house through the kitchen door. I picked the chair back up. I turned on the water, fluffed in some soapsuds, and began to wash the dishes. I bet Uncle Lamar hated me. Would he really make me leave? Was I gonna be homeless now? I wished Aunt Limo was here. She'd tell me what to do.

I could hear Miz Arzalia's voice in the living room, talking about a petition—to close Snake down. "You don't have many names on here," Uncle Lamar was saying.

I stopped washing to go to the door and listen.

"That's because Snake paid people to side with him," I heard Miz Arzalia say. "Gore told me that when we have drugs and crime as bad as in New York, then he'll sign. If we have to wait till we get as bad as New York, Silver Dollar Road'll be through! By then New York'll be cleaned up and Deacons Neck'll be the crime capital of the world. I don't want Silver Dollar Road even to get as bad as Dunbar and Carver Street in Myrtle Beach or Garvey Avenue in Gumbo Grove. It's too bad right now, and we should be fighting it right now. People everywhere else are trying to clean up their neighborhoods. What are we doing? Nothing!"

I heard papers rattle. "I can't sign this, not until Limo signs," Uncle Lamar said. "It's her brother she's gonna have to go up against. You know how she loves her baby brother, and she's crazy about Zambia. I'm crazy about her too. But, Arzalia, I did a terrible thing a little while ago. Zambia and I got into an awful argument over her father, and I told her some things I promised myself I never would."

"It probably was what she needed to hear, Lamar," Miz Arzalia said. "Sometimes *some* kids can make you say and do all kinds of things to them, trying to get them to do right."

I could hear Uncle Lamar's voice, low again, but I couldn't tell what he was saying. Could he still like me after the stuff I'd said to him? I went back to the sink to wash the dishes and try to think things out.

"No matter how bad things get?" I heard Miz Arzalia ask.

There was silence. Then I heard Uncle Lamar's voice. "We've all been down this same road before. It was Limo and her 'blood is thicker than water' business that kept Snake out of jail before. I don't know what it'll take to get her to change her mind."

C • H • A • P • T • E • R

9

I couldn't think. My insides churned like I was going to throw up. Nowhere to go. Nobody to talk to. Nobody around who cared. Maybe if I had some crack I'd feel better. Wasn't that why people did drugs anyway, to make them feel better? Was that white stuff around Snake's nose cocaine? Had he been feeling bad? I heard Uncle Lamar and Miz Arzalia leave. After I finished the dishes, I went out the back door and circled around to the front, and looked around for some dropped crack.

When I didn't find any, I sat down on the curb. For once the street was quiet, the way Saturday afternoons used to be before Snake opened his club. I didn't even see Potsey or anybody who looked like they might know how to get me some crack.

"Zambia!" That was Aretha, hollering from the house—no, *their* house. "Zambia! Phone! Lupe!"

"You okay?" Aretha asked after I came in.

"Why would you care?" I said, and was sorry as soon as I said it. Aretha sucked in her breath and turned away. I picked up the telephone receiver. "What?"

"Just why were you sitting in the road?" Lupe asked. "Trying to get run over?"

"Lamar beat me up and told me to leave and I don't have anywhere to go and not even my own father wants me around." I started to cry again. "He beat me up and called me stupid and told me to leave."

"Daddy didn't beat her up!" Aretha cut in on the kitchen extension. "They got into it over Uncle Snake, and Daddy only shook her 'cause she was hollering at him."

"Get off the phone!" I yelled.

"Well, tell the truth, Zambia," Aretha yelled back. "Lupe, she told Daddy she hated him, and—"

I banged the receiver down to try to disconnect the line, but that didn't work because I could hear Aretha still talking. Maybe I should go knock her down to shut her up. Doubling up my fists, I took a step toward the kitchen, then stopped. What was I doing? I slumped down on the couch instead.

I saw Lupe come up on the porch. "Hello, I'm coming in. You should start locking your doors. A house on the next street got emptied down to the walls overnight. Somebody backed up a truck to the house and took everything. Nobody was home and the door wasn't locked."

She sat down on the couch by me. "What's up?"

I shook my head. Tears jumped out of my eyes. "He looked awful and he had white stuff around his nose and he laughed at me."

"Who? Your uncle?"

"Snake. Snake. Lupe, I . . . yeah, Aretha's right. I told Uncle Lamar I hated him." I told her about the fight. I even told her how I had looked for crack. Lupe rested her arm around my shoulders. Aretha poked her head in the door, but she didn't say anything.

"You went crazy up here today, and they went crazy down there last night," Lupe said after I had calmed down. "Last night three fools got out in front of the nightclub, okay? Two of them held the other one by the arms and feet and swung him between them just like he was a big jump rope. Two or three others jumped back and forth over him. Next, two women got into a fight in front of our house and cut each other. Then somebody overdosed on something and had to be driven to the hospital by Mr. Grey from the funeral home."

My throat was sore from the tears. "All this happened last night?" I whispered. "You got an eyeful, huh?"

"I wish I hadn't. This stuff ain't fun, Zambia. I saw those women cut each other up bad. It was . . ." She shook her head. "I got sick. I used to think it'd be hip to be around a club, like how we loved to go on Garvey Avenue and stare at stuff happening at your daddy's club over there. But now Momma and I can't even sit on our own porch at night anymore 'cause we might be shot by a stray bullet or somebody might come up on the porch and get us."

Aretha slipped in and sat down. Nobody said anything again. I took a deep, shaky breath and tried to think of something to take the talk off me and Snake and people getting hurt. "I meant to ask you where Potsey got his beeper. It looks cool."

"No, it doesn't," Lupe said through her teeth. "Potsey's hanging around with these weird guys from out of town. I can't say exactly what he's doing because I haven't seen him do it, but all of a sudden Potsey's got new clothes, jewelry, that beeper, and thick wads of hundred dollar bills. Daddy found money in Potsey's closet this afternoon, and they had a big fight. Potsey threatened to hit Daddy, and told him to keep the money 'cause he'd get more. Momma doesn't know 'cause this happened while she was at work. So it's been awful at my house too. It's gonna get worse when she comes home and finds out."

A chill went down my arms. I told her about the vial Potsey'd grabbed off the ground. "Yeah, well, that's not the half of it." Lupe let out her breath like air coming out of a balloon. "Promise me you won't tell a soul. You promise, too, Aretha. I know Potsey's selling crack, or imitation crack, or something. I *know* it. I found two little bags with little brown rocks in his blue jeans pocket. It could be brown sugar, but I'm scared to taste it and find out. He's gonna get killed."

She stood up. Her eyes were red. "I gotta go back. I ran up here 'cause Aretha said you sounded like you were about to go off. I hope you guys are gonna be all right." She looked from Aretha to me. " 'Cause I got too many problems at home to be running back and forth trying to keep you guys straight too."

She went to the door. "And I don't know how you'll like this, Zambia, but it's your daddy making everybody fight each other."

"I can't do anything about what my father does."

"You're finally realizing that?" Lupe said. "Welcome to the real world. 'Bye."

I sat quiet. I still felt lost.

Aretha spoke up. "You still hate me and wanna leave?"

"No, girl. I never hated you. But I don't even know if I can stay here, after . . . after everything."

"Daddy doesn't want you to go," she said. "Zambia, you made Daddy cry when you said you hated him. I saw him, in his car."

I kept my eyes down at the floor. "I didn't mean it." Her telling me that sunk me lower than my feet. Uncle Lamar crying?

"Daddy's never done anything mean to you. You ought to apologize to him for saying all those nasty things. I mean, if you really are sorry and really do want to stay here."

"He did call me stupid, remember?" I said.

"You are," she said back. "You said Uncle Snake laughed at you, and called you stupid too."

I flinched.

Saturday evening I sat on the couch looking for the courage to apologize to Uncle Lamar. When I heard his car crunch into the driveway, I lost my nerve and ran into our bedroom. "I can't look him in the face. I'm gonna feel like a real bumhead for the rest of my life."

Aretha tore a piece of paper from her diary. "Then write it down."

I sat down at the dresser. "Dear Uncle Lamar," I wrote, and that was as far as I got. What if he laughed at my letter? What if he didn't believe me? I really was sorry. But how could I let him know I meant it? I looked at the picture of Momma. Had she ever run away from home? I bet she'd be ashamed if she knew how I'd acted today. I felt as low as a worm.

There was a knock on the door. "Come in," said Aretha.

Uncle Lamar walked in with his cap in his hands. He looked worn out. "Zambia."

"I'm sorry!" I burst out crying. "I don't hate you and I don't want to leave and I mean it, and I feel like dirt for talking so mean to you!"

I stared at the floor, sure he was going to say I was lying. When he didn't say anything, I sneaked a glance at him. Uncle Lamar was twisting his cap in his hands and wetting his lips. He cleared his throat.

"Thank you," he said. "I . . . you . . . I'm sorry too. I never ever laid a hand on you or Aretha before in my life. Aretha and you are my hearts, and Lord knows I don't want anything to happen to you." He let out a big breath, then walked over to me with his hand held out. "My home will always be your home, sis. Shake?"

I was so relieved that instead of shaking it, I grabbed his big, warm hand and rubbed it against my cheek. His hand smelled like peanuts. Uncle Lamar pulled me up and hugged me. Then I felt Aretha beside us, hugging me too. I didn't feel so ashamed anymore.

"Let's not forget what happened today," Uncle Lamar whispered, "and not let the bad parts happen again. Go on to bed now, girls, and get some sleep."

As I lay in bed with my eyes puffy from crying so

much, my thoughts kept bouncing from my uncle's warm handshake and hug to his angry words and shaking me. Then I'd think about my dad letting me work for him and squeezing my hand. But there were also my dad's broken promises and his laughing at me that I had to deal with. Who was right?

Just as I was finally about to fall off to sleep, I heard *chunka, chunka, chunk.* I struggled to come back awake. There it was again, a truck engine, revving right under my window. Peering out the window, I saw a truck with some people in it parked in our front yard under our security light.

"Aretha, wake up! Come see!" I tiptoed to the living room to get a closer look. Laughing and hollering, a white man and a woman hopped out of the truck. They broke out a six-pack of beer. Loud music came through the truck window.

In the living room darkness, moving toward the front door, was Uncle Lamar with his shotgun in his hands. Meanwhile the people outside were stuffing newspapers into Uncle Lamar's barbecue grill. The man lit the papers.

Uncle Lamar flew out to the front porch. "Get outta here!" he yelled and pointed his shotgun at them.

The people weaved back and forth a little around Uncle Lamar's grill while the paper burned like they hadn't even heard or seen him.

"What the—? Hey!" Uncle Lamar waved the shotgun at them.

But the man took a sip of beer, then held the can out to Uncle Lamar. "You Lamar? Your brother-in-law name Snake? He said we could come up here and cook some chicken on your grill, 'cause all the grills at his place are full. It won't take but a minute. You can have some. Hope I didn't wake you all up. You got any barbecue sauce?"

Uncle Lamar let out a stream of cuss words and fired that shotgun—*Boom!*—up in the air. Man, those folks jumped back into that pickup truck and flew out of our yard. Uncle Lamar stamped back into the house and locked the shotgun away. Mashing his cap down on his head, Uncle Lamar left the house and charged down the street toward Snake's nightclub.

In a few minutes I heard *Bam! Bam! Bam! Bam! Bam! Bam! Bam!*

"Were those gunshots?" I yelled. Aretha and I ran out of the house in our bed shirts to the sidewalk in the hot, humid night. Dozens of cars lined the streets, and people streamed in and out of the club. A police car with its dome light spinning flashed past us and stopped in the street in front of the club. A crowd of people pushed up around the car.

"What're those cops doing up there?" I said. "Coming into our community, causing trouble."

"Shut up!" Aretha snapped.

I shrugged. "Well, isn't that what happens on TV? Something happens, then the cops come in and everybody—"

"This isn't TV, Zambia! Daddy's down there," she said.

Folding her arms across her chest and pressing her lips together, Aretha walked fast back into the house.

Her words sent a shock through me. I sat down on our steps, and rested my head down on my arms. I hadn't thought about Uncle Lamar getting hurt. Nobody would hurt Uncle Lamar, would they? Nobody, except those folks he'd just run off his property. My daddy was down there too. Would anybody dare hurt Snake?

My stomach started to churn like it had right after the argument with Uncle Lamar. Why couldn't I stop and think about real people getting hurt?

After what seemed like hours, the police left and the people in the street at the club thinned out a little. Way after midnight, it was Sunday morning now, but the club was still open. I didn't see any ambulances or rescue squads go up there. I went back inside the house and dropped into bed. Aretha was rolled up in a ball on her bed with her face to the wall. I sent up a little prayer that Uncle Lamar—and Snake—would be all right.

When the screen door slammed, Aretha and I jumped up. We staggered out of our beds in Sunday morning's pink dawn and wobbled into the living room. Uncle Lamar slumped down on the couch, yawning. He pulled his cap off his head.

"So, are you okay, Daddy?" Aretha said, wringing her hands. Her eyes were red.

"You didn't get shot or nothing, did you?" I added.

"I'm okay," he said. "I went into that place to see Snake, but he hid up in the back when he saw me come in. That joint is like a zoo, and he's the caretaker. Drunks, drug dealers, pimps, prostitutes, addicts, kids, old people, white folks, black folks, Indians, Mexicans—they're all packed up inside there and around in the streets. I even saw a preacher from Myrtle Beach. He'd just got some drug dealer out of jail." Uncle Lamar snorted. "Preacher talking about 'He's a good boy, he just ain't got a job.' Here I am, working two jobs, but I'm making a living. I don't need to sell drugs to make money." He stopped.

"What else happened up there?" Aretha said.

"A guy got stabbed over some drug deal that went sour," Uncle Lamar said. "He ran off before the police could help him. Some kid, I think. People fighting and showing off their guns. Selling drugs. When these creeps get run out of one spot, they just pop up in another."

He closed his eyes and folded his arms. "I'm going to sleep. Don't let me go past seven-thirty, hear?"

We sat there and listened to him snore. "I wonder who it was that got stabbed?" Aretha said after a bit.

"I'm sure glad it wasn't him. Sure hope it wasn't Potsey." Then I remembered something. Sure hope it wasn't Snake, either, I told myself.

C·H·A·P·T·E·R

10

As soon as Uncle Lamar woke up Sunday morning, he went to the hospital to try to bring Aunt Limo home—if the infection in her leg had cleared up enough. We wanted to go with him, but he told us to stay and straighten up the house real good for her. We even thought about going to Sunday school, since it was Sunday, but we didn't. I did send up a prayer that Aunt Limo would feel better, and guess what? She did! She came home and let us fuss over her and settle her down in their bedroom. Aretha and I stuck right by her all afternoon, glad she was back home. She even played a few short hands of Hearts in the bed. Uncle Lamar tried to play, too, but he kept falling asleep. Then he had to go off to his evening job.

Things were quiet Sunday night—the Paradise was closed. Not Monday night, though. That was "Monday Night Baseball at Snake's" with his big screen TV. His customers made bets on the game, and whooped and hollered every time there was a hit. Between innings, the jukebox would come on with loud music, and there was still lots of traffic. Uncle Lamar stood at the front door almost all night long, guarding the house—and his grill. I know because I got up to go look. He and Snake were up at the same time almost all the time now, but not for the same reasons. Luckily, Aunt Limo was so medicated that she slept through all the noise.

By Tuesday Aunt Limo was able to get around the bedroom a little on her crutches. By then Aretha and I were ready to get around too. When I thought she was awake, I got up my nerve and stuck my head through her bedroom doorway to talk to her about Uncle Lamar and me and her and Snake. But when I saw her face looking so peaceful, I asked instead if she wanted anything from the kitchen. When she said she didn't, I asked if I could go to Rev. Reed's for a pop. She said okay.

"And then when you get back, I'm going to the library." Aretha met me at the door. "They got some videos over there I been on the waiting list for for a month. Don't be gone long, promise!"

"All right, girl. But when you get back, then I get to go—"

"Just get gone now."

Mr. Shinshiner sat on his front porch in his wheelchair. Country music came from his little radio-TV set. "Need anything from the store?" I yelled.

"No," he hollered back, raising his cane, as usual.

As I headed toward Rev. Reed's, cars cruised up and down the street, blasting their music. Within less than a month, Silver Dollar Road looked and sounded like Garvey Avenue. Two men set speakers on the roof of a car parked in Snake's parking lot. By the time I was opposite the nightclub, the car radio was blasting soul music from radio station WWWP all over the neighborhood. I kicked my foot a couple of times to a song, but then I remembered Aunt Limo. I hoped that music wasn't keeping her awake.

Miz Arzalia came to her door. "Zambia, would you go ask those fellas to turn that music down?" she said. "I can't even hear my TV in the back room."

Remembering Miz Arzalia's old petition, I hesitated about helping her out, but then Mr. Shinshiner probably couldn't hear his music very well either. "Okay." A little nervous, I strolled across the street to the men. "That lady over there," I said, pointing, "wants you to cut your box down."

One of them spit a wad of gum on the ground, then flicked his cigarette down there. "Who are you to tell us what to do?" he said.

"Snake's daughter," I said back. "Quit trashing up his yard."

"Oh, yeah, yeah." He reached in through the car window and turned the music off. "No problem." He picked up the gum and the cigarette. "Okay? We're getting ready to leave too. I sure nuff don't want Snake mad at me. You Seritta or Meritta?"

"Zambia." I walked back toward the grocery store. Inside I was shaking. That dude was so big his fist could have smashed me flat to the ground. What if he'd pulled out a gun? Did he do what I asked because I was one of Snake's kids or because he was afraid of Snake? Probably wasn't because of me. I sighed. But at least I got that one little thing done.

At the grocery store Rev. Reed sat hunched over a

bunch of papers spread out on the countertop by the cash register. "Zambia, I remembered what you said and I did something about it."

I shook my head and backed off. "Uh-uh, not me, I didn't say it. Don't blame me."

"You forgot!" She pointed to a shiny red NO SMOKING sign hanging on the wall behind her. "Remember how you got after me for not practicing what I preached? So I stopped selling tobacco products. It was a hard decision to make at first, but later on I felt better. After all, I did have a choice. 'Course, Mr. Gore and a few of my other main customers were disappointed."

"Did they stop smoking too?"

"Heck, no. They said I was right to be health conscious and blah, blah, blah, but they're still puffing and chewing and dipping. Now they buy their cigarettes, chewing tobacco, and snuff someplace else, like at Snake's. So I'm losing money standing by my choice, even if it is the right thing to do."

"But that doesn't make any sense, to do something right that's gonna hurt you."

"It's only short-term hurt, because it made me think harder and now I got an idea. I plan to sell ice-cream cones and ice pops. Maybe the ice cream truck that you all run to won't get all those quarters and dimes."

Rev. Reed said she was going to try to get a loan from a bank, and turn the store into a full-time ice cream and cake shop, maybe sell sandwiches too. "Then I *can* hire some of you kids," she said. "Silver Dollar Road until about twenty years ago used to be Deacons Neck's black business district. Then it started going downhill. Ten years ago it just, well, collapsed. Maybe I can help revive it through this little shop." She smiled. "And I can teach you guys how to start your own businesses. . . ." She paused, staring. A couple of men, a white one and a black one, walked in, bought pop, and left.

"That's the kind of customer I get now," Rev. Reed said. "They don't live around here, they come in and go right back out, waiting for Snake to open up. Zambia, lock your house up all the time now. Places are starting to be robbed. We didn't have that before."

I bought some pop and started back toward home. I looked for the blood spots in front of Lupe's house, but I didn't find any. Six or seven girls in long black hair braids, sun visors, red sunglasses, and long, long pink fingernails roared past in a little white Grand Am convertible. They shouted and swung their arms in the air in time to the music. They roared into Snake's parking lot, and the driver hopped out, pulled at the locked door, then hopped back into the car and drove off. I guess they didn't know that he wasn't open this early on Tuesday afternoons.

Seeing those girls made me flash onto my mother. When I hit sixteen and had my own car, I'd go to Charleston and make those doctors let me in to see her. I'd take her for a ride in my convertible, like one those girls were in.

I wished I'd been in that car. It reminded me of the ride I'd had with Meritta and Seritta in Snake's van. Man, that had been really hip back then—when I thought I had a chance of living with them.

Aretha was waiting for me on the porch. When she saw me, she hopped on her bike and rolled out of the yard. "Momma's okay," she hollered, and was gone.

I took a deep breath and told myself that it was time to talk to Aunt Limo. I went into her bedroom with some orange juice for her, my heart thumping like crazy. Aunt Limo was sitting up, picking at the bedspread. "How're you feeling?"

"Better. Thanks." She took the juice and slipped two round green pills into her mouth. "How's the outside world?"

"It's okay." I swallowed hard. "But I'm not. Aunt Limo, you told me not to be a hardhead while you were gone, but I was, a little. Well, I was, a lot. So I guess now I'm gonna find out what it's like to have a soft behind."

"Something tells me that you might already know." Aunt Limo reached for my hand, then rested it against her chest. She closed her eyes and tugged at my hand. I scooted up on the bed and lay beside her on her pillow.

I didn't know where to start. I did feel better being right there with her, though. So I said that first. "And I don't want to live with nobody else but you all, ever," I added. Aunt Limo rubbed my arm, but kept quiet. I cleared my throat. "I guess you heard about the fight between Uncle Lamar and me."

"I haven't heard your side."

"I didn't mean to talk mean to him. I—that was wrong. I told him I was sorry. I still am, for real. But, like, I've always hated to hear him say bad stuff about my father all the time. These last few weeks he and Miz

Arzalia really dogged him bad. Snake's still my father, no matter what. But it's like I'm supposed to sit there and not say *nothing* 'cause they're adults and know everything."

"Yeah, bad-mouthing drives me up the wall too," she said. "Even when it's true. It's hard to know what to do sometimes when you get in situations like that."

I sat up, glad she understood. "Yeah, but then I really felt like a fool because after I take up for Snake to Uncle Lamar, Snake turns around and lets me down. See, after the argument I go to the nightclub 'cause Snake said I—I could live with him. Snake comes to the door looking really weird, talking all rough, and I ask him and he *lies* to me! Then he *laughs* at me—just like he didn't care *nothing* for me—like before. And he calls me stupid."

My head hurt trying to hold back tears. "Aunt Limo, I felt like a real bumhead for talking so nasty to Uncle Lamar, because when I didn't have anywhere to go but right back here, Uncle Lamar let me come on in, like before." Remembering the hurt in his eyes during the argument and his hug that night, I couldn't hold back my tears anymore. "My own daddy lied to me, but Uncle Lamar didn't. That little ole bit of money Snake gave me didn't mean nothing to him. But you guys have been there for me all the time."

"Your father has always put himself first, ZamBee, and expects everybody else to put him there too," Aunt Limo said. "Lamar loves Aretha, of course, but he loves you in a special way. He's tried to be an uncle *and* a father to you. We've always made it clear that Snake's your blood dad, but we've tried to show you that you have a choice as to whose ways you want to follow—his or Snake's. Lamar's a good man. Maybe he's pushed too hard trying to show you that when you make choices, sometimes you have to make sacrifices." She shook her head. "Shoot, Snake's never sacrificed anything out of making right choices, 'cause the choices he makes are only for himself. Snake is one hardheaded man. Uncle Lamar's an ex-alcoholic, and he's really had it hard fighting off liquor."

Aunt Limo said that being hardheaded ran on both sides of the family. "You got a double dose. I'm hardheaded too. We're both in a fix over your father. I know it's been hard for you, loving your mom, loving your daddy, and neither one's been much help for you. I love them too."

"So what are we supposed to do?"

She sighed. "We can love 'em, but we don't have to love what they do, for one thing. I can't keep standing up for my brother's wicked ways. We don't have to *do* what they do, for another. After that, I don't know what to do, ZamBee. You tell me."

I lay back against the pillow, thinking. "Uncle Lamar said that Snake got Momma on drugs. Is that true?"

"Ho, boy, here we go," Aunt Limo said. "Yes, he did. I don't want to sound like Arzalia, but I got to start way back, okay? Me, Snake, Lamar, Reverend Reed—she was just Stoney then—and some other teenagers all ran together in the early seventies. No, we weren't a gang. We were just country kids in little-bitsy, backwater, hayseed, dirt-road Deacons Neck with nothing to do but listen to the radio and pick tobacco. Until your momma got hooked on cocaine and heroin. And the person who gave it to her first was your daddy."

"So'm I a crack baby?"

"No. Understand that he didn't force it on her. She took it by choice. Anything that came along, Renelda'd be in line to try it out. We used to call her 'Miss One,' because she always had to be first. When she was eleven, she jumped off a seat on the Ferris wheel on a one-dollar bet. She got her dollar, but she also broke her right leg in three places. She was truly hard-headed."

My father's real name was Vernon, but nobody ever called him that, or even Snake. "We first called him Sugar, because he was so sweet," Aunt Limo said. "He'd bat his long eyelashes at you, talking up a storm, smiling. We'd think he was so sweet and look past what he'd done wrong. My baby brother, Sugar. He could sweet-talk his way out of everything."

As Sugar grew older, he learned how to get what he wanted for himself and anybody else. "I remember when Leon Gore—yes, Lupe's father—wanted this real expensive bike. Sugar went over to Myrtle Beach, stole it from a tourist, then sold it to Leon for thirty dollars. He bought beer for us, too, 'cause he looked older. He could get whiskey, gin, any kind of booze."

Aunt Limo said grown folks sometimes had him get booze for them, too, when the bars were closed on Sunday. "Which they shouldn't have, but they did."

Sugar and Renelda started going together. Their

crowd really moved fast then. Too fast, said Aunt Limo. "We already knew about booze. Then we discovered marijuana."

"You? Not Uncle Lamar!"

She nodded. "Us too. Pot wasn't any big deal. I puffed a few times, got hungry, and fell asleep. Booze has always been worse than pot. But that summer everything changed forever. Somebody bet Momma twenty dollars that she was too chicken to try cocaine. She said she'd do it if Sugar would get it, and of course, he did, from over in Myrtle Beach. She snorted a line, won her twenty-dollar bet, and got crazy as a bedbug," Aunt Limo said. "Nobody told us how dangerous cocaine was. I tried it once, your daddy did, Lamar too, but not Stoney. I have sinus problems to this day because of it. My right nostril burned like fire and bled for six days. I thought my whole nose was gonna drop off."

But Momma and Sugar and some others kept doing it. Then Sugar came along with some heroin for a bigger thrill, and Momma had to try that too.

I hated needles. "Why'd he keep getting that stuff? Why couldn't she just say no? How come nobody stopped them?"

"Stoney and I tried to help, but they were hardheaded, like you are, and wouldn't listen. Plus, your momma was trying to keep up with Sugar. He was good-looking, had a fine car, lots of money, and your momma loved him—but so did all the other ladies."

"Sugar was always thinking up easy ways to make money," Aunt Limo said. "Half of them didn't work. The ones that did usually were illegal. He taught your momma how to shoplift leather coats, high heels, and jewelry, then he'd sell the goods on the street in Myrtle Beach and Gumbo Grove. Sometimes they even sold stuff out in the street or from his car here when we had a little black business district. The street was starting to go downhill but nobody said anything.

"But when Sugar started selling drugs out here, respectable people got scared and stayed away. Most of the honest shops on the street had to close down for lack of paying customers. The barber shop, the grocery store, which has been in Rev. Reed's family for years and years, and one or two more, hung on. When a guy tried to open up that bar, everybody finally got together and ran him off to try to save what was left of Silver Dollar Road. Sugar left, too, and went to Gumbo Grove and Myrtle Beach. It's been quiet over here ever since. Until now.

"One night, hopped up on rum and Coke and cocaine in some lowlife hole on Carver Street in Myrtle Beach, your momma and Sugar got into a horrible fight," Aunt Limo went on. "He hit Renelda, then she cut him with a broken beer bottle. That was how he got the scar, and the nickname 'Snake.' "

She patted my leg. "I was right there to see it. Awfulest thing I ever saw. When I carried him to the hospital, he made me say he'd been in a fight with a man. See, they were arguing and he actually called her a snake first. So Renelda told him that she'd put her mark on him as a reminder, and she did. Everybody started calling him Snake after that. That scar kind of looked like a snake too. He hated that nickname, but it stuck."

When they broke up, Sissy from Myrtle Beach came along, Aunt Limo said. Renelda lost Snake and her supplier, and Snake lost his partner in crime for a while. "Snake and your momma got back together, but he became very cold, like his new name fit his new personality," she said. "And Renelda got wilder. The sad thing was that they actually did love each other."

Aunt Limo said Momma and Snake had been smart students, but they dropped out of school. Rev. Reed, Aunt Limo, and a few others made it through. Uncle Lamar quit school with his alcohol problem and went into the army. When Momma got arrested for shoplifting a blouse from a Gumbo Grove department store, Stoney Reed and Mrs. Reed, her mother, got her out of jail and returned the blouse to the store. The store dropped the charges.

"But Renelda's father—your granddaddy, Reverend Ephraim Brown—whipped her with a wire coat hanger when she came home," Aunt Limo said. "He and your grandmomma, rest their souls, knew Renelda was in trouble with drugs. They'd known it for years, but refused to make a move because in their eyes she could do no wrong. Until she got arrested and got their good name dirty. So instead of getting that girl some treatment, they kicked her out of the house."

Momma moved in with the Reeds, but she stole stuff, so they made her leave. "Next Renelda moved in with Sugar and me and Momma and everybody," said Aunt Limo. "This was before I was married. I was still home. Sugar wanted her there, and our mother—your other grandmother—couldn't say no. Shortly after that you came along."

Renelda and Snake did okay for a while, Aunt Limo said. Momma was trying to get off dope and trying to take care of me. She even had a little job at the doughnut shop. "You and Renelda lived with Snake and us for about two years. Your momma did try, Zambia. Snake even kind of tried too. At least—"

"You mean I did live with my father?" That was news. I guess that helped me feel a little better. "But something had to happen, huh?"

Aunt Limo nodded. "Well, he was still stealing, concealing and selling stolen property, and dealing drugs—right out of our house! My momma knew this was going on right under her nose, but Snake was giving her money, and he *was* her baby Sugar. So she protected him."

After Uncle Lamar got shot in the army and came home, he and Aunt Limo got married and moved into this house. They'd been engaged since ninth grade, she said.

Somehow Renelda found out that Snake was still carrying on with Sissy and was the father of Seritta and Meritta, and taking better care of them than her and me. "That was what broke your momma's heart," Aunt Limo said. "They had another big fight, Renelda and you moved out of the house, and she went back to heroin, drinking, and shoplifting. She lost her job. She took you over to Myrtle Beach and you all slept on the beach almost all summer. Sometimes she and you slept in that old abandoned apartment house on Carver Street that a church owned. She fell in with some low lifes over there and that's where she started getting her drugs again. I'm sure that's where Renelda got hepatitis."

Aunt Limo thinned her lips. "I see some of those folks from over there, singing in the choir, still running drugs. I know that she tried to get help from one of those churches and the pastor wouldn't help her 'cause she wasn't a member. I'm not blaming the church about that; I'm blaming the pastor. But the bottom line is that Renelda didn't have to live like that. She had a choice. She didn't have to drag you around. She could have come stayed with us and turned herself around. But she didn't. I don't know. Maybe she couldn't. But she could have tried."

Poor Momma. I wish I could have been old enough to have helped her. But then I remembered when I'd been out in the yard looking for crack, and how I'd felt trying to find something to make me feel better too. Now I knew that what I wanted sure couldn't be found in the street. Look what happened to poor Momma.

Aunt Limo stopped. She sighed. "Anyway, we did persuade your momma to let me and Lamar keep you in the winters. Your momma wouldn't stay. Her liver was acting up from all that drinking even then. She'd pop in to see you. I remember one time in February she hitchhiked over here from somewhere, came in wearing a big black fake fur coat, high heels—and shorts! She'd brought you a valentine. She loved you."

That went on for a couple of years, getting worse

and worse. Aunt Limo said Momma was arrested three more times. Then the police found Momma in a pharmacy she'd broken into, just about dead. She had drunk a bunch of liquid medicines and taken all kinds of pills.

Aunt Limo and I sat quietly for a few minutes. I wished I could remember Momma and me doing something together. After Momma's last arrest, the social services people tried to have me placed in a foster home, Aunt Limo said, but Uncle Lamar fought like a bear to keep me. Momma was placed in a psychiatric hospital.

"Now she hardly even talks. This past year I haven't been able to make myself go down to see the poor thing, but I *do* call every week."

"ZamBee, it hasn't stopped. Seritta's running drugs and stealing stuff for Snake. She and Meritta and their momma are so busy dealing they can't see straight."

She pursed her lips and gripped my hand hard. "Zambia, I got to tell you this, and it's not good either."

"What else can be going wrong?"

"The nurse told me last month that Renelda's got AIDS. It was probably in her system when they first took her in, but nobody knew anything about AIDS then. Or else she got it in the hospital. You can pick up anything in—"

"So she's gonna die soon?" I flopped back hard a couple of times onto the pillow.

Aunt Limo put her hand on my shoulder. "We're all gonna die, honey. They say she's not any worse now than she was before, but I think she's pretty bad off.

Lamar and I've had *that* on our minds too. We do need to go down there soon. This is near the end of July. Somehow we got to get you in to see her."

"No, I don't want to see her, not like that. I want her to be like in my picture," I said. "Smiling."

"I know," said Aunt Limo. "But she's made it this long. There must be a reason for it. The will to survive can help to keep you alive, you know. Even the worst bad things can be a blessing in disguise."

"What does that mean? Blessings and stuff're supposed to be good."

"It means that out of even the most horrible problems, when it looks like you just got nowhere to go and things just keep getting worse and worse, somehow, someway, somewhere there's a little bit of good that's gonna come out of it. But you gotta believe that it's there and you gotta hang on to it, 'cause that's what's going to keep you going and carry you through it, out of the bad and into the good. Reverend Reed told us that in one of her sermons. I gotta believe that it's true. I gotta believe it for your momma and Snake, and all this awful stuff going on around us."

"Then would that mean that she won't die?"

"No, it doesn't mean that." Aunt Limo sighed. "It could mean that you learn to deal with the things that happen to you, and keep on trying. This was an awful lot to have to tell you," she said, "but now you know the truth from somebody who loves you. You needed to know the truth so you can stop fantasizing about Snake, face reality, and move on."

Reality was that my mother was an alcoholic and a

drug addict and dying, and my father was a criminal, but it wasn't my fault, and I still loved them both. I wiped at my eyes. "But I guess you can't fantasize about Snake anymore either, huh?"

"What do you mean?"

"You just told me all this bad stuff about him, yet you haven't signed that petition, 'cause you love him. Shouldn't you face reality and move on too—like how you want me to do?"

Aunt Limo moved her hand from my shoulder to her mouth. She touched her lips with her fingers, then dropped her hand back in her lap. "Well . . . I . . . um. I don't know if I can, ZamBee."

"But if you can't, how can I?"

I slid off the bed and wiped my eyes, but they kept filling up. "I think I'll just go outside now for a while. You want anything from the kitchen?"

She shook her head. Through a blur of tears, I stumbled outside into the backyard to the storage shed, and huddling up behind it, bawled like I thought I was gonna die too.

C • H • A • P • T • E • R

11

From deep inside my head a thin siren wailed. I wished Aunt Limo had told me about my parents a long time ago. It sure would have saved me a lot of years of crying, like I was doing now. Why couldn't they have just loved each other? Sirens filled my ears and all around me now, but these sirens were real. Blue-and-white flashes of police cars whizzed past our house. Wiping my puffy eyes, I rushed to the front yard.

The police cars had stopped at Mr. Shinshiner's house. On the porch lay Mr. Shinshiner's overturned wheelchair. The begonias and geraniums that usually bloomed in their pots and metal cans on his porch railing now lay broken and scattered in the grass. Three cops ran up to the front porch and into the house. A small group of people had formed in his front yard.

Back from the library, Aretha was already over there. "I heard that two men dragged him out of his wheelchair and beat him all over his head with his own cane right out on the porch," she said when I reached her. "They took that little TV-radio, his wallet, and his gun. Somebody going by found him on the porch."

"That old man's never bothered anybody, not *ever*." I pushed my fists up against my face so people couldn't see my swollen eyes. "Who'd do this?"

"Someone crazy," said a man beside me. "Who else would jump an old man on his front porch in Deacons Neck in broad daylight? We're not supposed to have stuff like that happen here."

When a policeman on the porch touched the wheelchair, one of the back wheels slowly rotated. I focused on that wheel, trying to force a vision of Momma and Snake way back when, beating up old folks and stealing TV sets, out of my mind.

A red, white, and blue rescue-squad truck swung around the corner and rolled up to the curb. It was followed by Rev. Reed's old Ford. She stepped quickly up the sidewalk and entered the house. Three attendants jumped out of the truck with a stretcher and trotted in after her. Miz Arzalia picked up a begonia hanging half in and half out of its coffee can, and pushing the rootball back into the can, returned it to the porch railing.

The attendants carried out a stretcher with something on it covered by a white sheet. "Oh, my God," Miz Arzalia said. "Is that him? Is he dead?"

"No," the policeman said. "But I hope that preacher's got an extra strong prayer for him."

As they lifted the stretcher into the truck I heard Mr. Shinshiner moan. Then the doors slammed shut. Lights flashing, horn blasting, the truck carried Mr. Shinshiner away.

■

Aretha and I walked back home without saying much. I stayed outside on the porch to try to think. What if the robbers who beat up Mr. Shinshiner were some of Snake's customers? What if Mr. Shinshiner died?

I looked toward the nightclub, wanting to go wait for Snake. I had a bone to pick with him anyway about the way he'd laughed at me and lied to me. But first I'd ask him about Momma. Maybe he'd get so ashamed that he'd apologize for how bad he'd treated her. And then I'd tell him that he needed to make his customers behave. When I got through with him, maybe he'd stop selling drugs and make the neighborhood safe for everybody again. Then I'd talk to him about me. Maybe . . . yeah, right. I sighed. As if he'd listen to me when he wouldn't even listen to Aunt Limo.

Potsey rolled by, but not on his bike. He was in the minivan with Meritta and Seritta. I frowned. What was he doing with them? Aretha came out eating a peanut butter sandwich and dropped down beside me. "I'll be glad when the tourists leave the beach. Maybe things'll quiet down over here too," she said.

"Don't count on it. Aretha, I gotta ask you something. Promise you won't tell anybody else, okay? Promise?"

"Uh-oh. What did you do now?"

"Nothing. Just promise," I said, but Aretha shook her head. "Okay. I'll ask you anyway. Do you really think Seritta and Meritta're selling drugs?"

Aretha yawned. "Girl, I thought you had something *new* to ask me. Everybody knows they've been hanging in Deacons Neck almost every day since the club opened. First I see them both in the mall by the pay phones, then I see them in the club parking lot. I see a kid come up to Seritta in the mall, then they take off together. By the time I get back over here Lupe says Seritta, Meritta, *and* the kid have been at the club. Then I hear that Seritta's back at the mall with somebody else half an hour later. So you tell *me* what they're doing. They were into drugs in Gumbo Grove, anyway."

The van turned into the parking lot. "Now it looks like Seritta's got Potsey working with them too," said Aretha.

I started to say that maybe Seritta was just giving Potsey a ride because maybe his bike had a flat tire, or that maybe . . . Instead, I kept my mouth shut. Aretha went back inside.

I lay down in the porch swing and covered my face with my arms. I wished I could make my momma get well. I wished I could make Potsey get away from Seritta if she was really just going to use him for . . . for something wrong. I wished I could change my father around. I got so frowned up and frustrated I made my head hurt. Wasn't there anything I could do to make things better? Why couldn't I think of something?

By the time the eleven o'clock news came on Tuesday night, our street had filled up with honking cars, loud music, and voices everywhere outside. Aretha had to turn up the TV so we could hear it over the noise outside. Somebody had stopped their car near our house and left the music on while they went somewhere. That happened a lot now. I patted my foot in time to the music, then remembered Mr. Shinshiner and stopped. I hoped it was quiet where he was. I hoped it was quiet where Momma was too. There wasn't anything about Mr. Shinshiner on the news, though—just stuff about tourists, the ocean, and the tobacco crop. I sat by our bedroom window, watching and listening and trying to think.

Wednesday morning I woke to the telephone ringing, and Uncle Lamar's voice: "Limo, it just got worse. That was Arzalia. She said somebody broke into Stoney's grocery store and tore the place apart."

Uncle Lamar, Aretha, and I ran up there, and pushed past the people standing in the yard. The front door to Rev. Reed's grocery store hung lopsided, its screws pulled nearly out of the wood. The screen door lay on the ground, covering her crumpled signs. I was afraid we'd see Rev. Reed crumpled up too.

Inside the store I could see red patches of wetness trailed over burst bags of rice and beans, broken glass, and smashed cans on the floor. Please, Lord, let Rev. Reed be safe. How could I have ever wanted to see somebody shot, stabbed, or dead!

Rev. Reed walked out of the store just then. She was all right, thank God. She hadn't taken time to wrap her dreadlocks in a scarf like she usually did when she was out in public. Her dreadlocks rose up, then curved down below her face like thick brown bristly fingers.

"They threw ketchup and barbecue sauce everywhere," she told Uncle Lamar. "It really grieves me to know that people out there are so full of hate and suffering that they have to do this."

"Did they get any money?" Uncle Lamar asked.

"I never keep money overnight. That's probably what made them tear up the store so bad."

About that time a white policeman and a black policeman drove up. "All right, everybody, move back, move back," the black one said as he walked into the yard. He pulled out a notebook.

"With the station right around the corner, couldn't you have got here quicker than this?" Miz Arzalia asked. "She called a good half hour ago."

"They're too busy watching after downtown to bother with us over here, huh," Mr. Gore said to everybody.

The black cop turned his back on Mr. Gore and Miz Arzalia and faced the rest of us. "I'm Captain Dirk Vereen," he said, "and this is Captain Ralph Sutton. Is Reverend Stoney Reed here? Any witnesses to what happened?"

"Now, if I'd seen who did it, I'da gone after him myself," Mr. Gore said, looking around to see if anybody agreed with him.

Captain Vereen strolled over to Mr. Gore. "Buddy, it's time for you to shut up. Now, who's Reverend Reed?"

"I am. Let's talk at the church." She took each policeman by the elbow and guided them to the church parking lot, away from us. "I have insurance," I heard her say, "but not enough to handle all this damage."

Uncle Lamar turned to Mr. Gore. "You're doing all

this loudmouthing—why couldn't you say no when Snake came to you with that 'hush-hush' money in his hand?"

"Look out now," Mr. Gore shot back. "I—"

Uncle Lamar snapped around to Patrolman Green. "You've arrested Snake enough times to know what he'd do over here. Why did you sell him your lot?" He turned to the people around us who were listening and smiling. "I told all of you not to let that club open up again 'cause of the crime it'd bring back. But no, all you could see was Snake's hush money dropping into your little greasy hands. See what happened? Look at Shinshiner! Look at the break-ins, look at the drugs, right back up in our faces again."

People stopped laughing and began to mumble and growl at Uncle Lamar. Were these the same folks who Aunt Limo said closed up that guy with the bar here way-back-when and chased the criminals away? From what Uncle Lamar was saying and how they were reacting, they didn't seem like they were.

When Uncle Lamar snatched off his cap and threw it on the ground, his veins stood out on his forehead. What if he had a heart attack? "Uncle Lamar," I said real low and touched him on his arm. Aretha picked up his cap. She looked embarrassed, too.

"Calm down, Lamar," somebody said. "You don't want the cops to hear—"

"Yes, I do! That's why I'm naming names!" Uncle Lamar punched his big forefinger at Mr. Gore. "Gore, you wouldn't sign that petition 'cause you've let Snake sell our lodge bootleg liquor for years. Green, you're a cop supposed to uphold the law, yet you got a racket going with other cops, crooks, and judges. You arrest the crackheads, then you help get them out on bond, then you pay the judges to let them off easy. Everybody all over the country's fighting crime, but you folks sit back in Deacons Neck acting like you don't see a thing."

Bert Green folded his arms. "I wouldn't talk about what anybody else is doing, not when your own wife offered to put up her house money to help her brother buy that lot. That's what Snake told me. He must be okay in her book, especially when you know he's got the cash to pay me outright. She won't sign the petition either. Why haven't you? Or does your wife tell you everything to do?"

"Put up the house money?" Stepping back from Bert Green, and looking puzzled, Uncle Lamar slowly took his cap from Aretha. He took his time settling it on his head. He jerked his head at us to follow him, and walked away from everyone. Behind our backs, I heard people laughing, and folks saying, "Hey, Lamar, what house money?"

"This is awful," Aretha whispered to me. "And I bet it's gonna get worse when we get home."

When we got home, Uncle Lamar strode into the bedroom to Aunt Limo, and closed the door. Pretty soon we heard them arguing. Trying not to listen, Aretha and I hurried into the kitchen, poured ourselves some orange juice, and flew out to the front porch to see and hear what was going to happen outside. I had to talk to Snake for sure now.

Aretha picked at her thumb, then bit at the nail. "I wish they'd stop fussing. I wish all this stuff would stop."

"Well, Aunt Limo said that the same bad things will happen to each generation, and that each generation has to fight the bad stuff off."

"Sounds like something Momma'd say," Aretha said. "But why couldn't some generation a long time ago have just gone ahead and had one huge fight and got rid of all the bad stuff for good, so *we* wouldn't have to deal with it? It's not even eight o'clock in the morning and already a store's been broke up and people are fussing, and I still got the washing to do."

"I bet it's gonna be a long day," I said.

Uncle Lamar pushed open the screen door and, letting it slam shut, stamped out onto the porch. "You can teach a baby right from wrong, but Snake hasn't been a baby for a long, long time," he yelled back into the house. "Here I am, a black man, your husband, fighting against wrong, trying to help you raise these kids right, and here you are fighting against me. I got some pride too. Choose him or me is all I got to say."

I watched him march down the steps to his old Datsun and get in. "Good-bye," Aretha said, and I waved. He nodded at us, then backed out of the driveway. We went inside to see what Aunt Limo was doing. She was sitting on her bed with her leg stretched out. Her little toes stuck out of the end of the cast. Her eyes were puffy now like mine had been.

"You need your medicine?" I asked. "Or something to eat?"

She shook her head. "Some peace of mind and some common sense are what I need," she said. "Girls, if you don't remember anything else I ever say to you, remember what I'm about to tell you, okay?"

"Yes, ma'am," Aretha said, and I nodded.

"Number one: You can't please everybody. When you try to please everybody, you end up not pleasing anybody, especially yourself. I know, because I'm caught between a rock and a hard place right now because of it. Number two: Stick to the path that the good Lord has set out for you, and everything else will fall into place."

We said okay. But just as I left the room, I heard Aunt Limo say, "Now if the Lord will just show me that path."

Wednesday washing called Aretha. The kitchen floor called me. "What'd you think Aunt Limo meant?" I asked Aretha as I helped her sort the clothes.

"Like maybe Uncle Snake's the hard place and Daddy's the rock and Momma's gonna stick with the Lord? I don't know. I feel like I'm waiting for something else awful to happen, and it's not even noon."

"Me too, but I sure hope it doesn't happen to us."

Just as I finished cleaning up the kitchen, I saw through the window Snake's blue minivan roll past. Seeing that Aunt Limo was asleep on the couch, I hopped out the door just as the van went into the club parking lot. I headed toward the club. This was going to be my path, I told myself. I just hoped everything would fall into place, like Aunt Limo said.

When I got up there, though, I stood across the

street for at least five minutes trying to get up my nerve to talk to my father. What if he laughed at me again? While I worked on my speech, Seritta and Meritta—instead of Snake—came out of the club. I waved at them, relieved and disappointed at the same time.

"How're you doing, sis?" Seritta asked, and, smiling, strolled across the street to me.

"Hey." I smiled back. "I sure like that belt you got on."

Seritta unbuckled the gold chain belt. "Then it's yours."

"Really? Thanks!" I strapped it right on.

"Have mercy," said Meritta, watching us from the club yard. "Am I gonna have to teach you how to dress too?"

"Uh, no, not with shorts, ZamBee," Seritta said. "Have you seen Potsey lately? No? Well, if you do, tell him I need to talk to him. You can be my Silver Dollar sis today."

"Sure, right." Helping Seritta! At least Seritta never laughed at me. She always seemed to include me somehow. I liked the sound of that. Maybe Aunt Limo would too. Maybe this, and giving me her belt, would show that Seritta wasn't the kind of bad girl Aunt Limo thought she was.

"Look, I know you want to make some money, right?" Seritta lowered her voice. "Tell you what. If anybody comes around asking for me today, say: 'Number Two's back by the wall.' Got that? Especially Potsey. That's all you say. I'll give you twenty dollars for every person who tells me that they heard those words from you today. Don't tell Meritta, though. She'd try to cut in on our action. You got it?"

"Right. 'Number Two's back by the wall.' What does that mean?"

"None ya," she said. "Remember, this is just between me and you."

I repeated the message, proud and suspicious at the same time. Twenty dollars a pop! This couldn't have anything to do with drugs. I was just passing along information, right? No big deal. Going back to the house to get my bike, I refused to look at Rev. Reed's boarded-up grocery store. When I checked at the house, Aretha was still washing clothes and Aunt Limo was still asleep. I rode up and down the street to see if anybody wanted me to tell them where Seritta was.

By three o'clock, loud music blared from cars, while others did doughnuts or drag raced up and down our street. At least six guys stood out on the sidewalk and under trees waving at cars, flashing finger signals and hollering "Yo, man. Yo, sister." A couple of them waved at me to come over, but I lost my nerve and rode on home. I don't think they were looking for Seritta. I didn't like the way they looked either. Who were all these people on Silver Dollar Road? I wondered if our street had looked like this way back when. I tried to imagine guys on the sidewalk rushing up to cars, trying to sell the pants, shoes, and coats in their arms, like Aunt Limo had said.

Potsey finally rolled toward our house on his bike. Relieved, I flagged him down.

"I hope you got something good for me," he said when he reached me.

"I do." I cleared my throat. " 'Number Two's back by the wall.' That's from Seritta. I'm working for her now."

Potsey leaned back on his bike, fingering two gold chains around his neck. "Say what?" he asked. "C'mon." He got off his bike and began pushing it up the street toward his house as we talked. "So did Seritta tell you to tell me that—*Seritta*, by name, told you to tell me that?"

"What? Yes . . . no . . . well, she's the one who told me. What's it mean?"

"You don't need to know. Later, ZamBee. I got business to do." He touched my cheek. "Girl, you get cuter every day."

My smile got big as a barn. "Let me hang with you, please?"

"Okay, as far as my house." We walked up to his house, talking. When a car went by and a guy hollered, "Yo, Deuce!" Potsey raised his fist and signaled the guy.

"Deuce? What'd he call you that for?" I said.

" 'Cause the deuce is wild, like in cards. I'm the Deuce, wild in real life. Plus, Potsey is a baby name. You ask too many questions." Potsey locked his bike to the porch pillar. "Here we go. Later, sweet thing."

"You got to let me hang with you longer than this." I rubbed his back tire with my fingers. "I can do business too."

"In your dreams. You could barely tell me what Seritta said."

"Boy, you'd be surprised what I can do. I can be your—your Silver Dollar sis, your good luck charm. C'mon. I know what you're into. I can make you roll seven every time."

"Listen to you talking trash!" Potsey laughed. "So what'm I into?"

I started to tell him what Lupe had told me, but I didn't want to get Lupe in trouble. "Remember that vial you took that we found? That's what I mean," I said instead.

Potsey shrugged. "Oh, that's nothing."

"If there's nothing to see, let me come help you do your business."

"Okay. Come on, but no more questions. No babies need apply."

"I'll show you who's a baby," I said. Potsey's long legs moved fast down the street to Strom Thurmond Highway. I had to trot to keep up with him. "ZamBee, I'm gonna be rich one day," he said. "I got the perfect plan."

"I know. You're gonna be Cinque, the Afro-Hispanic weight lifter."

"Naw, I can do that when I'm old. I got a plan for now. Dig, when I go over to Myrtle Beach or Gumbo Grove, the tourists always ask me how they can cop pot, crack, cocaine, gold chains, women—stuff like that. I used to get mad because it was like they figured I was automatically supposed to know. When I told my old man he just said not to pay them any mind."

We walked along Strom Thurmond Highway, passing tractors pulling loads of tobacco. A kid driving one tractor stuck his forefinger and thumb out at Potsey, and Potsey did it back.

"You got to tell me what that means, Potsey." I was tired of all that secret finger flicking. I bet it stood for something wrong.

"You ask too many questions. You wanna hear this or not?"

I shut up.

Potsey tapped his temple. "So I started to think how I could turn those jokers out and make some bread too. The Snake knows how to get all that stuff they want, see. So now when they want something I check with Seritta, and she gets it through him. Okay now. 'Number Two's back by the wall' means that Seritta—Number Two—is at the phone booths at the mall. So I call her there and set her up with who wants to get whatever."

We passed a truck full of stinky pigs. I pinched up my nose and listened harder to Potsey. "Sometimes she says 'Number Two's at the beach,' which means she's at the pavilion by the phones. Or 'Number Two's at the Dollar,' which means she's on Silver Dollar Road. Understand?"

I shook my head and slowed down, trying to figure it out. "Sounds like what you're doing's against the law."

"Not me." He shook his head and dusted his hands. "I don't see or touch a thing. That's the beauty of my plan." He raised his big shoulders. "I don't carry anything and I don't take their money. I just get a cut from the person wanting the stuff, and another cut from Seritta for getting Snake another customer. We're businessmen."

"You and Seritta's stealing and dealing, you mean. Potsey, it's still against the law! You—"

Potsey spun around to face me. He slapped his hands against his chest. "Scared, little baby? Go home."

"I'm not scared," I lied. "Not crazy either." I turned around to leave, hoping he would follow. "I got to go, uh, Deuce. Come walk me home."

Potsey turned his back to me. "Shouldn't told you nothing. I thought we had something coming together. I thought you were fly like Seritta, but you're still just a baby."

"Hey, I'm so fly, I got wings." Things were going the wrong way. "I'm Snake's kid too, you know."

"You don't act like it. You can forget that ole jive stuff they tell you in school about right and wrong," Potsey said. "Remember what happened to me for bringing my machete? It was right for other kids to bring their knife collections, but wrong for me. Now I know how it goes. If it works and you don't get caught, then it's right. If you get caught, then it's wrong. Don't you know that by now?"

"Sure, sure." But that wasn't what Aunt Limo and Uncle Lamar and Rev. Reed said. Did Potsey know something that they didn't?

"So was it right for somebody to tear up Reverend Reed's store and beat up Mr. Shinshiner?" I asked.

"No, but probably somebody needed what they had and took it. Law of the jungle."

"But they didn't really have anything, Potsey; we don't live in a jungle, and Mr. Shinshiner wasn't bothering anybody."

"Then he was in the wrong place at the wrong time."

I put my hands on my hips. "On his front porch?"

Potsey held up his palms to me. "Back to you and me. I been trying to rap to you all summer, and just when we're finally starting to spin, now you wanna back off."

"What do you mean, spin?" My heart beat faster. "Spinning with Seritta is what I'm seeing."

"I told you I don't want Seritta—I want you." Potsey pulled me up against him. Next thing I knew he was kissing me on the mouth, hard and long. He let me come up for air. Whoa!

"So are you gonna be in with me? You ready to spin?" He came at me for another kiss. I hung on like I was getting oxygen. A couple of cars honked at us. We pulled apart.

"Potsey, what you just did . . ." was all I could think of to say. My lips burned from the pressure of his lips against mine. My heart beat faster than it ever had before. First kisses! Right at the corner of Ninth and Strom.

Potsey stood with his legs spread apart, sandwiching mine, his big hands around my waist, his head cocked to one side. "Well?"

"What? Oh, Potsey, I . . . Potsey, I . . . yeah, sure, I'm in. I'll spin."

C · H · A · P · T · E · R

12

As the crowd thinned in the busy lobby of the Silver Dollar Festival Mall, I saw Seritta leaning against a telephone booth. Her smile for Potsey dissolved when she noticed me.

"All you needed to do was just tell him," she told me when we reached her. "You didn't need to come too."

"She's with me," Potsey said. "She's all right."

Seritta, though, frowned up, huffing and puffing, didn't look like *she* was all right. She stopped long enough to answer the ringing telephone. After speaking into it briefly, she hung up. "Go home, sis," she said to me. "I'll square up with you when I get back over to the club, promise. For now, go home."

"But I'm with Potsey," I said.

That got her all frowned up again. She whispered something to Potsey, who pulled me out the lobby doors. "You don't want to make Seritta mad," he said outside. "She's my business partner, and yours too, now. You gotta do like she says."

"Then what's with this whispering in your ear, and her not wanting me around, if we're all in business?"

Potsey laughed. "Oh, that. Seritta doesn't like a lot of people knowing her business. And she likes us to do just what she says. Now listen. I gotta meet a chump in a couple of minutes. He's Seritta's customer, but I'm gonna use a plan on him that Seritta told me she got from the Snake himself. This chump wants ten rocks, see, but I'm gonna get his money and he won't get a thing. He'll be driving a little white car. We get in his car. He gives me some bread for the rocks. I take him to my house. You get out of the car with me. We act like we're headed to the side door to get the stash, but we go on down the alley and chill until the chump leaves. That's all there is to it. Classic scam."

"Wait a minute. I want to make sure I get this straight. You're not gonna give this man the rocks and he won't get his money back either. Right?"

Laughing, Potsey nodded.

"But won't he want his money back? Won't he want to kill us? What if he calls the cops?"

"And tells the cops what?" Potsey raised his shoulders. "That he's trying to buy some crack? I won't have *no* drugs, remember? Well, I give him a sample, but it's mostly baking soda and brown sugar, so that doesn't count. He's gotta give me a deposit, see. That's my take. Or maybe give me all the bread up front. If it came down to it, it's the chump's word against mine. This is a perfect plan. Nobody ever comes after me."

"You mean you've done this before?"

"Sure." He looked away. "See, I'm like Robin in the 'hood, taking from the rich and giving it to the poor—me! Sometimes I take 'em to other houses, then split.

They be knocking on people's doors, mad, looking for me."

"Robin in the 'hood, huh? Is that how Mr. Shinshiner got beat up?"

"Huh, I don't know *nothing* about that." A white sports car drove past us slowly and stopped. "There's the chump. You don't like this plan? You think it's dumb, huh? You don't think I'm smart, do you?"

"Oh . . . uh . . . yeah, you're smart. The plan's . . . uh . . . all right. I know I sure want it to be, Potsey. You're the smartest boy I know, Deuces."

Potsey puffed out his chest and pumped his arm muscles. "That's right, my sweet little good luck charm. Deuces wild, man. Let's do this thing. Keep your mouth shut. Trust me. I'm in charge."

Wednesday afternoon traffic was picking up in downtown Deacons Neck, and so was my nervousness. This deal didn't sound right, and I didn't feel right about it. But like Potsey said, I had to trust him because he was in charge—especially if I was going to be his girl.

The frowning guy driving the car stared at us hard. He took a drink from a plastic cup and belched. "How do I know you're not just selling soap?"

"Go wash with it," Potsey growled back. "Look, are you on or off?" The man nodded. When I froze, Potsey pushed me into the backseat and got in. The stink of sour beer and cigarette smoke in the car curdled my stomach. Potsey gave him directions to Silver Dollar Road, and we drove off. A little red Mustang roared up quick behind us, then veered off. "Who was that?" Potsey asked. "In that car."

"Who was who?" the man said. "Where's the stuff?"

"How much you talking about?" Potsey said.

"Enough not to have to deal with no more punks like you again. Gimme a sample."

"Gimme some money."

"You're nuts. Gimme the sample first."

I slid down a little in the seat in case fists started to fly. After the guy handed Potsey some money and Potsey handed the man something, I relaxed a little and sat up. So far, so good. My stomach settled down a little. When we reached our street, Potsey pointed out his house, and the man drove up to it. Potsey opened the car door. "We'll be right back."

"This stuff tastes weak," the guy said. "Gimme another one." He swung his arm over the seat toward me. "No, gimme the girl till you get back." Potsey jerked me out of the car. I stumbled onto my feet. We ran through the backyard and down the alley. The man hollered behind us.

"Potsey, he's gonna kill us!" I cried.

We ducked behind Miz Arzalia's chicken shed. "Potsey, is he coming? We're gonna die!" I stuttered against his back. The chickens clucked and squawked inside.

"He can't find us." Potsey's voice cracked. "Look, I got us some money. Not much, but something. Twenty bucks."

"Twenty bucks!" I bit my fingers to keep from scratching him instead. "We almost got killed over twenty bucks?"

Potsey peered from behind the building. "I don't see him. We're okay. Look, the dude was supposed to give me all the dough up front," he said. "He said so on the phone to Seritta. He lied to me though." He turned around and leaned back against the wall, and wiped his sweaty face on his T-shirt. "This was the Snake's plan, anyway. Seritta said he saw it on a TV show."

My mouth fell open. "TV show? How did it end?"

"I don't know. Happily ever after?" Back to his old self, Potsey flashed that grin at me. "Here, take the money, ZamBee. Call it your cut, from the Deuce."

"I don't want a cut, Potsey. What if that guy's still out there?"

"Well, he's not. Nobody's here but me and you." Potsey pushed the bill down in my shirt. I snatched it back out.

"Potsey, we're in trouble. We—"

"Shut up." Potsey pressed me up against the chicken shed and kissed me again and again. He tasted like cigarette smoke. I clutched the twenty-dollar bill in one hand, a handful of his T-shirt in the other. Finally Potsey let me loose, breathing hard. I frowned, giggled, frowned again.

"You're beautiful, ZamBee." Potsey tried to kiss me again, but I pushed him away. "I know. I'm greedy. So meet me up on my porch around seven," he whispered. "Maybe I'll take you over to Snake's back room and we can party. You're the Deuce's girl for real now, right? Right?"

It felt like my tongue was stuck to the top of my mouth. Rubbing at my mouth, I only nodded at Potsey.

Potsey walked a few feet up the alley and looked around. "It's okay. Later, ZamBee. I got to get back—to work." He started to leave, then stopped. "And next time, nobody'll mess with me, 'cause I'm gonna have a gun. Later, ZamBee."

My whole body felt sticky, and I wanted bad to brush my teeth. Was this how Momma and Snake had got started? Were Potsey and I gonna be like them, all over again? Potsey with a *gun*? The odor from the chicken coop and the tobacco taste from Potsey's kisses swooped over me. My cheeks got warm and my stomach rolled. Leaning against the shed as the chickens clucked inside, I threw up. When I could stand straight, I struggled home.

Scrubbing in the bathtub and brushing my teeth helped. Putting on fresh clothes and Seritta's belt did too. I was able to even smile a little about Potsey's kisses. I had the boy of my dreams, and I just had my first kiss. This was going to be one day that I'd remember forever. I couldn't smile about the scam, though.

"Zambia," Aunt Limo called for me from the front porch. "Come out and talk to me, honey."

"Why?" Did she know about me and Potsey making out? Had the police come to arrest me for that scam? I took my time going out there.

She patted the porch swing. Slowly I came out and sat down. Her crutches leaned against the wall. "I signed that petition," she said. "It won't put your daddy in jail, but maybe it'll close down his club. Miz Arzalia's going around again to get more folks to sign. I can't take the noise, the robberies, and the drugs any more. It's tearing our neighborhood apart again, and it's tearing our family apart again. I let Sugar wrap me around his finger one too many times. Especially since he lied to Bert Green about the house money, and embarrassed Lamar like that."

I nodded. "I guess it's like you can love 'em, but you don't have to love what they do, huh, or go along with it either."

Aunt Limo's face brightened. "I'm so glad you understand. ZamBee, don't let people use your love to make a fool of you. This ole world's so darned screwy, but don't you let it screw you too."

I nodded and looked away. Could she see the shame on my face from the scam? Had I already screwed up? Should I tell her about Potsey and the gun? I handed Aunt Limo the twenty-dollar bill. "What's this for?" she said.

"Nothing. A present. Just take it."

"Where did it come from, ZamBee?"

"I . . . Potsey gave it to me," I said real low. "But I don't want it."

"Potsey? I've seen him with Seritta lately and I've already told you what she's into." She looked at me so sadly that I wanted to cry. "See how these things can flash through a family and burn everybody? That's what I mean by you having a choice, honey. It'd kill me to see anything bad happen to you, too. Potsey's a good kid. He shouldn't be with Seritta."

I lowered my head. Aunt Limo, stop! Aunt Limo held up the bill. "It's not like you to give away money. So why'd Potsey give it to you?"

"Because . . . because . . . Aunt Limo, he just did. You take it or . . . or throw it away! I gotta go!" I jumped off the porch and ran down the sidewalk.

"Go where? ZamBee, come back!"

I couldn't. Something had taken hold of me and pushed me off that porch, and was dragging me up the street. I had to *do* something—now! Should I talk to Lupe first? She would understand. But what would I tell her? That her brother and I had scammed a guy? That he planned to get a gun? That I was a runner for Seritta?

As I walked toward Lupe's, trying to think of what to say and do, the street began to fill with Snake's Wednesday evening business. Cars cruised up and down playing loud music. More strange guys held down spots on the sidewalk as I passed. Looked like everybody who'd been run out of the other towns had come over here, like Uncle Lamar said.

"Shake it, girl, and gimme some," a guy said. I wouldn't look at him or answer. Instead, I speeded up.

Maybe I could tell Potsey and Seritta and Meritta that having money wasn't worth having if you had to do wrong things to get it. Look what it did to my mom, I could say. Maybe I could get up a petition for kids against crime. Would they listen? Would they sign? Would they stop doing what they were doing? Why should something so simple to say be so hard to do?

A red Mustang rolled around in Snake's parking lot as I walked closer to Lupe's house. That's when I saw Potsey, Seritta, Meritta, and Lupe standing on the sidewalk in front of the Gores' house. Seritta and Lupe stamped around each other, flicking their hands in each other's face. I slowed down.

"I said I don't know *nothing* about this," Seritta was shouting at Lupe. "You call me over here to front me off on Potsey's lie!"

"My brother doesn't lie!" Lupe hollered. They circled each other again, shouting.

I sucked in my breath. I guess Lupe knew *something.* Lupe spied me. "Zambia, you stupid fool!"

Seritta jumped around and charged toward me. "Didn't I tell you to go home from the mall? Didn't I?" She punched me in the shoulder. "Were you and Potsey scammin'?" She snatched me around by my arm, tripped me, and knocked me down. "I ought to kick you butt. Maybe then you'll learn to stay out of trouble."

Potsey pushed at Seritta. "Leave her alone. It was my idea," he said. He reached down to help me up.

"And what're you doing scamming on *me?*" Seritta swung at Potsey.

"You guys gotta stop all the way around!" As I struggled to my knees, the Mustang swung around in the street, then roared toward me. I raised my right arm up.

Pam! Pam! Pam! Pam! Pam! Pam! Pam! Pam! Pam!

Fire tore into my shoulder and knocked me flat. The last thing I remembered was the scorching pain, and someone screaming, "Oh, God, they've killed them all!"

■

"Hey, sis," said Uncle Lamar. Every inch of my body ached with the effort of trying to open my eyes. When I finally did, his face came into focus, then Aretha's and Aunt Limo's.

"How you feel, baby?" Aunt Limo asked.

Their faces were the best things in the world for me to see. I shook my head a little. My right shoulder jabbed with pain. When I remembered why, tears trickled down my face. "Where's everybody? How's Potsey and them?"

"Meritta didn't get hurt. Potsey and Lupe're here in the hospital," Aunt Limo said. "They're . . . well, Lupe's all right. Potsey's not so good."

"Oh." I must have dozed off again for a few minutes. "Where's Seritta?" I asked after I came to. "Is she okay?"

Aunt Limo didn't say anything for a little bit. "Honey, it didn't go so good with Seritta," she finally said. "She . . . she died on the way to the hospital."

Seritta? Dead? I didn't even get to say good-bye. I went out again. When I woke up, Aunt Limo was rubbing my cheek. She had to tell me again about Seritta. And then the whole story. "When I heard the shots, something told me *you* were in trouble," she said. "I don't know how I got down that street to you on these crutches, but I did. When I saw you stretched out on the ground, I just about died myself."

"You must be hurting pretty bad," Aretha said. "Want me to call the nurse and get you a pill?"

"Yeah," I whispered. "Where'd they shoot Seritta?"

"Don't think about that part," Uncle Lamar said. "She's at peace now. And you're alive."

I focused on Aretha's face. She could have been out there and got shot too. About the only thing that made any sense was that Aretha was here, and so were Aunt Limo and Uncle Lamar. But Seritta was dead. A big part of my family was gone forever.

"Everybody was screaming and crying afterward," Aretha said. "There were a million cops everywhere, and TV cameras. Aunt Sissy was falling out over Seritta. Uncle Snake was trying to get her up. Meritta was sitting on the curb by herself, crying. Momma was hitting people with her crutches, keeping people off you, Miz Gore had Lupe in one arm and Potsey in—"

"Aretha." Aunt Limo shook her head. "ZamBee, did you see who did it?"

"Somebody in a red car, I think," I whispered. "Is it night?"

"This is Thursday, the next day," Aretha told me. "You've been out for over twelve hours."

Wherever Seritta was now, I hoped she wasn't scared. I hoped she hadn't been in a lot of pain when she . . . when it happened. Tears rolled down both sides of my face.

"Why would anybody want to shoot you guys?" Aretha asked. "You all were just standing around, right?"

I glanced at Aunt Limo. "I don't know why. I mean, I don't think I know."

Uncle Lamar looked hard at me. "What do you

mean by that?" When I didn't answer, he added, "Your father wants to see you. He's out in the waiting room."

"I don't want to see him. He made Seritta get killed," I said. "He made all this bad stuff happen in our family."

"Don't say that," Uncle Lamar said. "We'll be a family forever, no matter what. We're in this together. Seritta . . ." He shook his head and trailed off.

"I still don't want to see him."

"Well, you are, if only for my sake," said Aunt Limo. "He's already lost one daughter, and almost lost two more. It won't have to be long." She and Aretha and Uncle Lamar went out the door. I turned my face to the wall away from the door and away from *him*.

I heard my father come into my room and sit down in the chair beside my bed. We didn't say anything for a good five minutes. Finally I heard him shift in the chair. "ZamBee, I'm sorry you're hurtin'," my father said.

I didn't say anything. He didn't say anything else.

Finally I couldn't stand it anymore. "Seritta's dead, and it's all your fault," I said to the wall.

"Yes, it is. Yes, it is."

At his confession, I made myself look at him. Gray stubble was on his face. Sunglasses hid his eyes. His hair stuck out a little on the sides under his Panama hat. He didn't look sharp today. He just looked like an old man. "I'm gonna find out who offed her. She was a good kid. She was straight up."

"She was teaching Potsey how to scam, and how to deal dope," I told him. "She had me running messages. Potsey ran a scam that backfired and while she was fussing with Potsey about it somebody in a red car shot us. I know because I was with Potsey on the scam and I saw that same car follow us.''

Snake leaned forward in the chair. ''What scam? Potsey?''

Tears seeped out the sides of my eyes. ''You laughed at me when I asked you if I could stay with you, remember?''

Snake didn't move.

''All this time Potsey and I thought you were so big-time and I wanted to be just like you and Seritta, and I believed everything you guys said, but you told her stuff that got her killed. You're the one who told Seritta about this perfect plan you saw on TV and Seritta told it to Potsey and Potsey tried it and it didn't work, and now Seritta's dead. You gave Momma drugs and you make Aunt Limo cry. You make Uncle Lamar stay up all night. And you don't care nothing about me.''

''I care about you! I . . . Seritta . . . I saw that stuff on a cartoon. I was joking. And Seritta believed . . . ? Ahhhhh.'' He sighed real long and loud. ''And you hate my guts.''

''No, I don't hate you. You're still my father, no matter what. Aunt Limo said a person could love somebody but not have to love what they do.'' I closed my eyes.

''Well, couldn't nobody be hurting more than me right now,'' he said. ''I'm . . . sorry. I feel like I shot you all myself.''

The room was quiet again. When I opened my eyes, I saw Snake hunched over in the chair, the way Mr.

Shinshiner usually sat in his wheelchair. I guess he felt my eyes on him, because he straightened up. He lifted a gold chain, the one with the tiny snake charm on it, from his neck and placed it in my good hand.

"Keep this to remember me by." He stood up. "I know it probably don't mean much to you, but take it anyway. I don't know what else to do. Be good." And then he was gone.

As he went out, a nurse came in with a needle and gave me a shot. More tired than I'd ever been before in my life, still holding my father's chain, hurting in my shoulder and in my heart, I drifted off to sleep.

On Saturday I was able to go home from the hospital. Lupe had already been released. Potsey was still in intensive care. As Aunt Limo drove me home, I couldn't look toward Lupe's house, or at the nightclub either. I kept Snake's necklace wrapped around my good hand.

Aunt Limo and Aretha got me settled into bed. "This town has finally woke up again," Aunt Limo said. "People at last are admitting that Deacons Neck, just like everywhere else, has a crime problem too, and that it's past time to do something about it—again. People've been calling me all day and all night, wanting to know what to do. I told them to call the mayor."

Aretha brought me some lemonade. "After the shooting, Daddy got so upset that they had to give him a tranquilizer. Then he and Rev. Reed started calling up people all over the state to come over here and help us like they've been doing in Charleston and Columbia and Gumbo Grove. Rev. Reed even called the White

House for the president, the U.S. attorney general, and the surgeon general. She called the governor of South Carolina too. And then she called a press conference and announced a march for today."

"A march? What kind of march?" I asked. It was good to be back in my own bed again.

"A Unity in the Community march," said Aunt Limo. "We got you home just in time. That's why we pushed your bed right up against the window. You'll be able to see real good. It'll be live on TV too."

Aunt Limo sat down on my bed. I could tell that she had something else to say, so I waited. Seritta's funeral would be on Monday, she said. It would be up to me as to whether I felt like going. "Do I have to?" I asked. The thought of seeing Seritta dead sent my stomach jerking. "Are you going?"

"Oh, yes," she said. "She was my niece. We should be there for Seritta, to see her through to her final resting place. No matter how much it hurts, honey, that's what it's all about. Snake'll need us there. Sissy, Meritta too."

"Then I guess I gotta be there too." I gripped her hand tight. The tiny snake charm in my hand pressed hard into my palm. We didn't say anything else to each other. There was nothing else to say.

"Aunt Limo," I finally whispered. "Do you think Momma might hear about me being shot?"

"That's another thing." Aunt Limo sighed. "I don't know whether to call and tell her or not. I don't want to upset her."

"Well, I think I want her to know that I'm all right,"

I said. "She might have heard something on the news, and maybe worry."

"Oh, that'd be so good for her, to hear your voice," Aunt Limo said.

"Are you gonna be all right by yourself?" Aretha asked. "While we're at the march?" When I nodded, she added, "Well, I'm gonna come back home when it swings around here again. You might fall out of the bed or something."

She and Aunt Limo left, and I was by myself. I could feel a thick, sad quiet in the house, but I wasn't scared. I clicked on the television set with the remote control, and concentrated on looking out the window. Pretty soon I heard people chanting.

Through the window I saw Uncle Lamar and Rev. Reed march by holding a big red, black, and green banner that read UNITY IN THE COMMUNITY. A banner behind it carried by some other people read SAVE THE FAMILY. Behind the banners were Aretha, pushing Aunt Limo in a wheelchair, Miz Arzalia, the Gores with Lupe, and a bunch of other folks. Lupe had her arm in a sling. She, Aretha, Aunt Limo, and Uncle Lamar waved at me when they went past. With my good arm I waved back. On TV I saw our house in the background as the marchers, shouting, went past with their fists raised in the air. It was the longest line of people I'd ever seen on Silver Dollar Road.

"What do we want for this community?" Rev. Reed's strong voice rose up on the television and through the window.

"Drug free! Drug free!" the marchers hollered back at her.

"When do we want it?"

"Now!"

Striding along, her still uncovered dreadlocks bouncing in time to her voice, her pastor's red and black robe flapping around her ankles, Rev. Reed shouted out her questions, and the people roared out their answers.

Carrying signs that read NO MORE SHOOTINGS! and NO MORE CRIME, it seemed like every black person, and many whites, too, had come to Silver Dollar Road. They marched from the police station around the corner up our street, down another, over to Strom Thurmond Highway, back to Silver Dollar Road, and then to the Paradise Number Two.

Just then I heard Aretha's key in the front door lock. Sweating, she sat down quietly on my bed and watched the TV with me. "How do you feel?" she said.

"I'm okay," I said. "Glad to be back home."

"Glad you're home too," she said back.

Singing and waving their signs, the TV showed the marchers gathered in the yard of the club and in the street. My father stood in the doorway of his Paradise with his arms folded.

Rev. Reed charged right up to the door of the nightclub, her face only inches from Snake's. Uncle Lamar joined her.

"What do we want for this community?" she yelled.

"Drug free! Drug free!" the marchers hollered.

"When do we want it?"

"Now!"

"Why do we want it for the community?"

"To save our kids and our town!"

"Let us pray." Rev. Reed dropped to one knee, with one hand open, waving in the air. "Lord, let us pray for our children, for our community again, and for our lost daughter, Seritta LaRange."

After Rev. Reed finished praying, Miz Arzalia's voice rose up. "Somebody prayed for me," she sang. The marchers took up the chorus.

Aunt Limo, on her crutches now, hopped slowly to the door of the club and stood next to Uncle Lamar. "My sister prayed for me," she sang, and the marchers sang that.

She followed it with, "My children prayed for me," and the marchers sang that too. I saw my father put his fist up to his mouth. He closed the door of the club.

Poor Snake. It must have been terrible for him to know so many people were mad at him on the one hand, yet so many were praying for him—and Seritta—on the other. I was glad I told him that I didn't hate him. He was still my dad, and I still loved him too. I sent up a prayer that he'd be all right, and that Momma and Potsey would be too. Rest in peace, Seritta. I closed my eyes and drifted off to sleep.

ABOUT THE AUTHOR

A Blessing in Disguise is Eleanora E. Tate's third novel in a trilogy of books whose setting is Calvary County on the coast of South Carolina. Its sister books are *The Secret of Gumbo Grove*, a *Parents' Choice* Gold Seal Award winner, and *Thank You, Dr. Martin Luther King, Jr.!*, a National Council for the Social Studies–Children's Book Council Notable Children's book, and a Child Study Association Children's Book of the Year. She is also the author of *Retold African Myths*. Her book *Just an Overnight Guest*, which was made into an award-winning movie, is a companion to *Front Porch Stories at the One-Room School*, an *American Bookseller* Pick of the Lists. Also a journalist, Ms. Tate is a former national president of the National Association of Black Storytellers, Inc. A native of Canton, Missouri, Ms. Tate currently lives with her husband, photographer Zack E. Hamlett III, in Morehead City, North Carolina.

